## "So, you and Dub have really bonded, haven't you?" Lucy said.

Jack stared at her. "You gave me an assignment, and I take my assignments very seriously."

"An assignment."

"Was that the wrong answer? Lucy, Dub is my buddy. What else do you want?"

"I want you to be very careful." Lucy said the words softly as Dub approached them with a grin on his face and a blue ribbon pinned to his chest.

She addressed the little boy. "Congratulations again, Dub. Great job with the scavenger hunt."

"Not just me. Mr. Jack, too." He grinned.

Lucy glanced from Dub to Jack. Though Jack's face remained impassive, his eyes sparkled with amusement.

"Here, Mr. Jack, this is for you." Dub handed Jack the heart-shaped stone.

Jack smiled broadly. "Thanks, buddy."

Lucy's heart melted. Oh, this wasn't good. What was she thinking? Soon Jack would go back to his life in New York. And little Dub would be left with a broken heart.

And he might not be the only one…

**Tina Radcliffe** has been dreaming and scribbling for years. Originally from Western New York, she left home for a tour of duty with the Army Security Agency stationed in Augsburg, Germany, and ended up in Tulsa, Oklahoma. Her past careers include certified oncology RN and library cataloger. She recently moved from Denver, Colorado, to the Phoenix, Arizona, area, where she writes heartwarming and fun inspirational romance.

### Books by Tina Radcliffe

### Love Inspired

### *Big Heart Ranch*
*Claiming Her Cowboy*

*The Rancher's Reunion*
*Oklahoma Reunion*
*Mending the Doctor's Heart*
*Stranded with the Rancher*
*Safe in the Fireman's Arms*
*Rocky Mountain Reunion*
*Rocky Mountain Cowboy*

# Claiming Her Cowboy

## Tina Radcliffe

Recycling programs
for this product may
not exist in your area.

**LOVE INSPIRED BOOKS**

ISBN-13: 978-1-335-42782-3

Claiming Her Cowboy

www.Harlequin.com

**Printed in U.S.A.**

What time I am afraid, I will trust in thee.
—*Psalms* 56:3

This first book in the Big Heart Ranch series is dedicated to John Croyle and the staff and children of Big Oak Ranch. Big Oak Ranch is a Christian home located in Alabama for children needing a chance.

"That they might be called trees of righteousness, the planting of the LORD, that he might be glorified."
—*Isaiah* 61:3

A great deal of thanks goes to my wonderful agent, Jessica Alvarez, for partnering with me on this exciting new series. Thank you, as well, to my editor, Giselle Regus, for her ideas, which ultimately led me to Big Heart Ranch.

# Chapter One

If Lucy Maxwell had learned one thing, it was that when life appeared to be going smoothly, it was time to listen closely for the other boot to drop.

Because it always did.

The attorney who stood at the head of the conference table, in his finely tailored suit, with his impossibly thick black hair and deep charcoal eyes, was definitely sigh-worthy. He even had a slight dimple when he smiled. Which he didn't do very often. Except for his off-center nose, with the scar at the bridge, he was perfect. It was a good thing she was not taken to sighing over near-perfect men with dimples.

The man was unfamiliar to her. After working closely with the Brisbane Foundation for several years, she thought she knew everyone. But not him. She would have definitely remembered Jackson Harris.

He began to speak. The icy disdain that laced his voice as he reviewed the last twelve months of charitable funding to Big Heart Ranch obliterated any fanciful thoughts in Lucy's head. Instead, she blinked to attention and sat up straight, adjusting her sundress and blowing her thick fringe of bangs from her eyes.

"After a lengthy consultation with the foundation accountants, I recommend a significant reduction in funding to Big Heart Ranch for the upcoming fiscal year," he concluded.

Lucy gasped at the attorney's words. The sound was loud enough to cause the board members seated at the enormous conference table to turn and stare. She fanned her damp skin with the meeting agenda. It seemed that the cool air had been sucked from the room, leaving it as sweltering as the Oklahoma summer outside the conference room windows.

Reaching for her water glass, Lucy took a long drink. If ever there was a need for divine intervention, it would be now. Big Heart Ranch's own budget for the next year could not be finalized until the foundation's donation had been secured.

She should have suspected something was up when her presence was requested at this meeting. Usually, the ranch accountant met with the Brisbane Foundation accountant. And it was generally a simple transaction. Not this time. This time the director of the ranch was invited to the meeting. Lucy took her director responsibilities seriously and had arrived early and eager.

The start of the meeting seemed a lifetime ago. Now her hands trembled as she set the glass back down. Lucy clasped her fingers together tightly in her lap and turned to the other end of the table, where the chief executive officer of the Brisbane Foundation sat.

"Mrs. Brisbane?" Lucy prompted.

Meredith Brisbane had paled beneath her silver coif. She cleared her throat and touched the pearls at her neck, as if to reassure herself she was still breathing.

"Lucy dear, I can assure you this is as much a surprise to me as it is to you. Though my nephew is newly appointed to the foundation, I am certain he has our best interests at heart."

*Nephew?* How had she missed that significant bit of information?

"However, through no fault of his own," Meredith added, "Jackson has a limited understanding of why we partner with your organization. I take full responsibility for this omission. Lucy, perhaps you could enlighten him on how funding to the ranch is utilized."

"Yes. Yes." Lucy nodded, while her mind raced. "I'm happy to."

After all, Big Heart Ranch *was* Lucy, and her brother, Travis, and her sister, Emma. They'd single-handedly built the Timber, Oklahoma, local charity for orphaned, abandoned and neglected children.

Lucy paused, her confidence waning. She could provide the smug attorney with numbers until the ranch cows came home. Like the fact that the average cost of raising a child was well over two hundred thousand dollars, and that the ranch was raising sixty children. However, something told her that Jackson Harris would not be impressed with numbers. What *would* get through to this man?

She blinked. Like the kick of a stubborn mare, out of nowhere, inspiration struck. Lucy smiled and turned to face him.

"Spreadsheets and PowerPoint presentations can't possibly show you the true heart of our ranch, Mr. Harris. The best way to understand the big picture is to come to the ranch. Spend time with us. I'd love to show you our ministry in action." She paused. "Of course, I'm happy to provide you complete access to our financials, as well. You have an open door to anything you need from us."

It was Jackson Harris's turn to show surprise. He opened his mouth, but before he could respond, his aunt chimed in.

"Why, Lucy, that's a splendid idea. I couldn't agree more. He needs to see the scope of the ranch's reach."

Jackson's gaze moved from his aunt and then back to Lucy. He narrowed his eyes. "What exactly did you have in mind?" The words were measured and precise.

Lucy scrambled for a plan. "Summer," she burst out.

"Summer?" The attorney tugged at the collar of his dress shirt.

"Yes. We're about to start our summer program at the ranch. It's our busiest and most ambitious undertaking of the year. Not only do we work with our own sixty children, but we invite the children from the State of Oklahoma orphanage in Pawhuska to the ranch for vacation Bible study at rotating intervals."

He adjusted his silk tie and said nothing.

Lucy continued. "We're about to start our annual series of old-fashioned trail rides and campouts." She flashed him what she hoped was a confident smile. "The summer events are capped off in August, with a black-tie fundraising gala hosted by your aunt."

Had she imagined his jaw tightening as he reached for his water? The board members seated at the table glanced away and carefully examined the paperwork in front of them. An awkward silence stretched for moments until a melodic ring filled the large room. All hands shuffled and reached for cell phones. Meredith shot Lucy an apologetic smile as she retrieved her own phone.

"I'm so sorry. I must take this." Phone in one hand, cane in the other, Meredith stood and wobbled precariously. As she reached out for the table ledge, her cane fell to the thickly carpeted floor with a soft thud.

Lucy jumped up in time to grasp Meredith's forearm and gently steady the benefactress.

Jackson was around the table and at his aunt's side in seconds. "Are you okay, Aunt Meri?" he asked. Genuine concern laced his voice—the first sign of humanity Lucy had seen in the man.

"Oh, my. Sorry to give you two a fright." Meredith glanced from Lucy to her nephew and frowned. "An inner ear issue, the doctor tells me. Sometimes I'm a bit off balance. This getting-old stuff is not for sissies."

"How are you feeling now?" Lucy asked.

"I'm fine. Thank you, dear. I simply need to remember not to stand quite so fast."

Lucy nodded as she picked up the ebony cane and handed it to Meredith.

Head held high, Meredith's measured steps were nothing short of regal as she moved across the carpet. The room remained silent until the door closed behind her.

Harris again turned to Lucy. The man's unflinching gaze was anything but warm and fuzzy. The dark brows were drawn into a serious frown.

Lucy glanced around the room. Had she missed something here? Why was he so irritated?

"Visiting the ranch is out of the question, Ms....." He faltered for a moment. Clearly, he'd forgotten her name.

"Maxwell. Lucy Maxwell."

"Ms. Maxwell, I can't—won't—leave my aunt."

Harris gathered up his papers and stood without sparing another glance in her direction.

Lucy folded her hands and willed herself not to panic.

The other boot had officially dropped.

"Jackson? Is Lucy gone?" Meredith asked from the doorway of the great room.

Jack turned from the tall window that overlooked the front lawn and circular drive. "If she drives a beat-up mustard-colored Honda, then yes, Aunt Meri, she's gone."

Lucy Maxwell. He shook his head. He'd never met anyone like her before. A sunflower. That was exactly what she reminded him of, with that cap of dark hair and round chocolate-brown eyes, along with a smattering of freckles on her golden face. A petite woman, she wore a pale yellow dress along with red hand-tooled cowboy boots. When she walked, the dress fluttered around her calves, capturing his attention, whether he liked it or not. And he did not. Con artists came in pretty packages too, he reminded himself. He'd been taken in once before, and even put a ring on her finger. Never again.

"When will you start at the ranch?" Meredith asked.

"Hmm?" He blinked and met her gaze.

"What are you thinking about?" His aunt smiled. "Lucy, perhaps?"

"What? No." He gave his aunt his full attention. "I'm sorry. What did you say?"

"I asked when you will be heading to Big Heart Ranch."

He paused for a moment at the question, planning his strategy. "I'm not leaving you to spend time observing a ranch."

"Oh?" She smiled. "Then you're approving the original donation amount?"

Jack crossed the room and put an arm around his aunt's thin shoulders. "Aunt Meri, you know you're my favorite aunt."

She chuckled. "I'm your only aunt."

He grinned. "True. And while you are as generous as you are kind, you can't give away the foundation money to every shyster that comes along."

Meredith gasped. Her sharp blue eyes blazed, taking him back to his childhood days of misbehaving and facing his aunt's wrath. She had never hesitated to serve up well-deserved punishment for his crimes. Jack took a step back when she straightened to her full five-foot-nothing height.

"Lucy Maxwell is not a shyster!"

"What do you really know about the woman, Aunt Meri?"

"What I know is that the bulk of the foundation's income is from mineral and oil rights. My husband inherited those rights from his great-great-grandfather, who was one-half Osage Indian. The foundation was set up to ensure that the funds were invested locally." She pinned her gaze on her nephew. "Big Heart Ranch is as local as it gets, and they are an investment in this community's future."

He wasn't going to point out that she hadn't answered his question. Instead, he tried another tactic.

"You've proposed nearly doubling the donation to this ranch. Why?"

His aunt narrowed her eyes and exhaled sharply. "Have you been talking to your father?"

"What makes you say that?"

"He's made it quite clear that he believes I'm not fit to manage the foundation. Oh, he thinks he's being subtle, sending you out here as in-house counsel, but I know what he's up to."

"Aunt Meri, Dad's concerned about your health, that's all."

She offered a harrumph at his words. "I'll tell you what I told him, Jackson. Vertigo does not equal diminished mental capacity."

"What about the chemo?"

"My treatments are completed and I've been given a clean bill of health by my physicians. The cancer is in remission. Shall we have my oncologist contact your father?"

"Aunt Meri, please don't get upset. The bottom line is I'm here as the foundation's attorney. Not to inspect a ranch in Timber."

"I don't see why you can't do both. They have

internet and telephones at the ranch, so you'll be able to stay in touch. My assistant has all the numbers. Besides, while the ranch is on the outskirts of Timber, you're still only twenty minutes away."

"Twenty minutes is forever if you need me."

She paused and gave him a hard, assessing glance. "What are you really doing in Oklahoma, Jackson? You've been in New York since forever. I have a hard time believing your father didn't pressure you to come out here."

"Not at all. Dad would never do that."

"Oh, please. Your father could talk a peacock out of his feathers."

He laughed. She was right, he'd give her that. Except the truth was more complicated. His father did want him to check on his aunt. It was a coincidence that Jack desperately needed a change of scenery.

"He told me the position was open, and you were vetting candidates. Perhaps it was… What's that saying of yours? A God thing."

Her expression said she didn't believe him for a second. "You made it clear once you left for college that you prefer the big-city skyscrapers over the red clay of Oklahoma. You've been gone a long time. What happened to make you quit your job and take on the foundation position?"

"Let's just say that I'm reevaluating my options."

"In my day, a man like you would have been

considered a catch. Why haven't you settled down, Jackson?"

"Aunt Meri, I'm not much of a family man."

"What does your fiancée say about that? Isn't she still one of your options?"

"That's over."

She slowly shook her head and glanced past him, out the window. "I'm so sorry to hear that. What happened?"

"Let's just say she was more interested in my wallet than me."

"Ahh, so that's why you're being so hard on Lucy."

"My personal life has nothing to do with Big Heart Ranch."

"No?" She cocked her head.

Silence settled between them. "What's going on?" his aunt finally said. "You've been unhappy for some time. I could tell from your phone calls."

He met his aunt's perceptive gaze. Was he unhappy? Or simply disenchanted and searching for something real in his life?

She frowned. "You always wanted to make a difference, Jackson. What changed?"

"Make a difference? Did I say that?" He scoffed. "If I did, then you're correct. That was a long time ago. What's changed is that I'm not an idealistic attorney anymore."

"I think maybe deep inside you are." She placed her hand on his arm. "Don't get me wrong, I'm glad to have you here, but as far as Lucy Maxwell and Big Heart Ranch are concerned, you couldn't be more off base. I still contend that you can't make a decision to cut off their funding without investigating the situation."

"Off base? I did my research. That ranch is a money pit."

She offered a sound of disgust. "That doesn't mean they're mismanaging the funds. I don't believe for a minute that anything shady is going on at that ranch, and I challenge you to find one bit of evidence to support your claim."

Meredith gripped her cane and walked to the wall of family portraits. Her hand trailed the ornate, gilded edges of the frames. A huge portrait of Jack's grandfather hung next to a smaller one of her husband, followed by another of Jack's father. She stopped at a painting of Jack with his twin brother, Daniel. They were nine years old, mirror images, with matching grins and dark curls. There, however, the similarities ended. Daniel was charming, outgoing and impulsive, while Jack was shy, hesitant and introverted.

A wave of sadness and guilt slammed into him as he stared at the painting. Twenty-five years had passed, yet nothing would ever be the same. Daniel was gone and it was his fault. He'd been minutes behind his brother that day and hadn't been able to save him.

"I miss Daniel," Meredith murmured with a

soft sigh. He was surprised when she turned and wrapped her arms around him in a loving hug.

The scent of his aunt's lavender perfume carried him back years. "I miss him, too, Aunt Meri," he whispered.

His father's words from when Jack left New York raced through his thoughts. *When we lost your brother and your mother left, your aunt was there for both of us. This is an opportunity for you to be there for her. She won't ask, but Meri needs help.*

He swallowed hard as he stared at his brother's smiling face. "I'll go to the ranch, Aunt Meredith."

Jack grimaced when he realized that the words had actually slipped from his lips. When his aunt's face lit up, he knew that it was much too late to take them back.

"Oh, Jackson, I knew I could count on you to do the right thing. I'll call Lucy immediately."

*The right thing.*

For a moment, he'd let his guard down and sentiment had strong-armed him. Jack took a deep breath. He suspected his orderly life was about to be blown wide-open, and he placed the blame squarely at the feet of Little Lucy Sunshine, the director of Big Heart Ranch.

# Chapter Two

"I need a favor." Lucy stood in the doorway of the children's therapist and child care director of the Big Heart Ranch office. It belonged to her sister, Emma.

"Good morning to you," Emma said. She tidied the bookshelf in her already immaculate office and turned to Lucy. "What sort of favor?"

"Can you handle my calls for a couple of hours? I have to start a new volunteer."

"Sure. Only because then I can remind you that you need to hire an assistant."

"Not going to happen."

Lucy glanced at a platter of chocolate muffins artfully arranged on a table. "You made muffins? Like you don't have enough to do?" She nodded toward the portable cribs set up in the back of the huge room. Inside, her twelve-month-old twin nieces slumbered, thumbs in mouth and bottoms in the air.

Emma shrugged. "So tell me what happened at the Brisbane Foundation yesterday."

Lucy grabbed a muffin and peeled back the paper. "Meredith said to tell you hello."

"Was that before or after she handed you a sizable donation check?"

"Things didn't exactly work out that way."

"What do you mean?"

"Meredith has a new attorney who hasn't approved the funding. I'm sure everything will be taken care of soon."

Emma sank into a chair and nervously fingered her braid. "Lucy, we need to finalize our budget. I don't understand what the holdup is. She sent us preliminary numbers weeks ago."

Lucy met her sister's worried gaze. "The attorney is doing things differently."

"Is Travis aware?" Emma asked quietly.

"Yes. But you know Travis. All he cares about is the cows."

Emma glanced at the calendar and cringed. "This puts everything on hold."

"I know. Which brings me to the other news." Lucy dusted off her hands. "Leo quit."

"What? Why? He's our best ranch hand."

"He was offered more money at a ranch in Driscoll. I simply can't match the offer."

"So we'll hire someone else."

"I'm not going to hire anyone until the budget situation is resolved. In fact, I may have to lay off staff if we don't get the Brisbane Foundation backing by the end of summer." She met Emma's gaze. "All expenditures outside of the day-to-day ranch maintenance are on hold."

"What about the gala? I've already placed deposits for caterers, waitstaff and flowers. Not to mention the entertainment. Meredith always funds the gala."

"The gala is low on my worry list. Let's try to focus on what's really important. The kids."

Emma nodded.

"The Lord has been the financial backing for Big Heart Ranch since day one," she said. "This is His ranch. These are His children. He will continue to provide more than we can ask or imagine. Right?"

"Right," Emma said. "I couldn't agree more."

Lucy took a bite of the muffin and glanced toward the parking lot.

"Was there something else?"

"Yes."

Travis stuck his head in the door. "That new volunteer is here, asking for you, Lucy." He offered her a conspiratorial wink.

"Thanks, Travis. I'll be right out."

"What was that all about?" Emma asked. "And who's this new volunteer?"

"Jackson Harris."

"Who is Jackson Harris?"

"Meredith's nephew and her new attorney."

"What?"

"Perfect timing, isn't it? He'll replace Leo."

"No one can replace Leo. He did the work of three ranch hands." Emma stood and walked to the window.

"All the same, we should be grateful to have the help for the summer."

"I'm confused. Why would Meredith's nephew agree to volunteer on the ranch when it sounds like he's opposed to giving us the funding?"

"His aunt is very persuasive." She turned to Emma. "No one is to know that he's from the Brisbane Foundation."

"Why does Travis know?"

"He was here last night when the call came through from Meredith."

"Why the secrecy?"

"Mr. Harris is vetting us. I want his experience here to be positive. He needs to know we have nothing to hide. It's the only chance we have that he'll change his mind."

"Is that him?" Emma asked.

Lucy peeked over her sister's shoulder at the tall attorney whose back was to them as he talked to Travis.

"Yes. That's Jackson Harris."

Emma chuckled. "Look at him, all shiny and new in his designer jeans, Italian leather shoes and that dry-cleaner-starched shirt. Lucy, why would you take on a city slicker?"

"I'm not in a position to be choosy."

"Can he even ride a horse?"

"Meredith says he can."

Lucy edged closer to the window. When Jackson Harris turned around, she caught her breath.

"Oh, my," Emma said, her face lighting up. "Well, I suppose you could do worse."

Lucy turned to her sister. "What do you mean, I could do worse?"

"The man is mighty fine-looking, that's for sure. And you'll be working closely with him all summer, dear sister."

"Don't get any ideas. *If* I was looking for a man in my life, it certainly would not be another temporary cowboy." She shook her head. "I have most definitely already been there and done that. And I have an empty house in the woods to prove it."

"Just remember that sometimes the Lord brings us what we need, not what we want."

Lucy tossed the muffin liner in the trash and dusted off her hands. "This discussion is over."

"Six weeks!" Jack Harris stood outside a log-cabin-style bunkhouse next to Lucy Maxwell, trying to digest her words. "Where did you get the idea I was here for six weeks?"

"Your aunt," Lucy said. "She called me last night and said you want the Big Heart Ranch experience, and that you'd be filling our ranch hand position for the summer."

Stunned, Jack rubbed a hand over his chin and closed his mouth when he realized it was hanging open.

"Do you want me to call her?" she asked.

"No." He shook his head. "Look, between you

and me, my aunt isn't as strong as she used to be. She thinks she is, but those cancer treatments have taken a toll on her overall health."

"Apparently, she's well enough to pull one over on you," Lucy murmured. Her lips twitched as she concentrated on the ground, creating a line in the dirt with the toe of her boot.

Jack's gaze followed. She wore the red boots, this time with jeans and a bright red T-shirt with the Big Heart Ranch logo on the front and the word Staff on the back. Once again, she reminded him of a bright flower. This time a poppy. He averted his gaze and considered her words.

Lucy had assessed the situation correctly. He'd been bamboozled by his seventy-year-old aunt. Aunt Meri was right about one thing: Jack had been away from Oklahoma for a very long time. Long enough to forget how stubborn his aunt could be once she got a bone between her teeth.

"For some reason, she's convinced I'll change my mind if I see the ranch up close and personal," he muttered.

"Why is it you constantly think the worst of Big Heart Ranch?"

"This isn't personal. I have a job to do as the foundation's counsel. And I happen to love my aunt. I'm simply trying to protect both interests."

Lucy stared at him, obviously biting her lip. The dark eyes glittered with unsaid words. It was clear he'd pushed her buttons and she was working hard to control her temper.

"You seem to think we've committed an offense," she said. "If so, what happened to innocent until proven guilty?"

"Shouldn't I be the one on the defense here?" he asked. "First, you fingerprint me like a criminal. Then you make me sign a release for a complete background check. Now you're telling me I'm stuck here for six weeks." He shook his head. "The kicker is that I get to do it while living with two other guys. I mean, come on. You must be kidding."

"You'll be living like all the other volunteers. Think of this as summer camp for grown-ups." Lucy looked him up and down. "As for the other, we're entrusting you to care for our children. Children who have already suffered more in their short lives than you can even comprehend. These are children who have been abandoned, neglected and even abused. This isn't kiddie rehab, Mr. Harris. They don't come here to be fixed. They come here to live a normal life. We are their life. We are their family. Forever." She paused. "Makes your trivial complaints seem insignificant, wouldn't you say?"

"Believe it or not, I did my homework, Ms. Maxwell. I understand the ranch mission statement."

She raised her brows.

"First Corinthians thirteen. Faith, hope and

love. Faith in God, hope for tomorrow, and unconditional love."

When her lips tilted into a huge smile, the effect nearly knocked him over. A guy could get addicted to a smile like that if he wasn't careful.

"You memorized our mission statement." The words were a hushed whisper. "I'm impressed."

"Somehow I doubt that," he muttered.

"A lot of prayer and thought went into that mission statement, so yes. I am impressed."

He offered a short nod.

She handed him papers from the clipboard in her hands. "A list of recommended gear you'll need for the summer. Oh, and the schedule and a map of the boys' ranch, girls' ranch and important facilities. Phone numbers are listed, as well."

Jack glanced down at the form on top of the papers. "What's this? Yet another form?"

"Waiver of liability. If you choose to ride our horses without the recommended safety helmet, we need this signed."

"Do you wear a helmet?"

"It depends on the situation." She met his gaze. "Oh, and by the way, other than me, only Travis and Lucy are aware you're from the Brisbane Foundation. You are simply a summer volunteer, as far as everyone else is concerned."

"So I'm undercover? Why the big secret?"

"I don't want anyone to panic, and actually, Mr. Harris, it's to your advantage."

"How's that?"

"If everyone believes you're part of the team, they'll be open and transparent while you're here."

"If you say so," he replied.

"I do." Lucy pulled out a key and opened the bunkhouse door before dropping it into his hand. "Welcome to your new home. This is bunkhouse number one. It has all the amenities you should need—coffeemaker, microwave. If you need something more, let us know. We'll vote on it at the next budget meeting. Of course, that won't be until after the foundation makes their funding decisions."

A smiling Travis greeted them at the door. "Hey, Jack. You're bunking with us? Great." He held open the screen. "Come on in."

Jack folded the papers from Lucy and put them in his back pocket as he moved into the living quarters. "You live here?"

"Only during the summer," Travis said. "It's easier than driving home after a twelve-hour day, so I moved my stuff over today." Travis tossed his black Stetson on a bunk and winked at Lucy. "Besides, it keeps the boss happy, because if the boss isn't happy, nobody is happy."

"Keep it up, little brother," Lucy muttered.

"Who..." Jack waved a hand at the other bunk.

"Tripp Walker," Travis said. "The horse whisperer. Doesn't talk much. If it involves horses, though, Tripp is your point of contact."

Jack nodded.

Travis looked from Lucy to Jack. "Madame Director giving you a hard time?"

"One might conclude that."

"Her bark is worse than her bite," Travis returned, as though she wasn't in the room.

Lucy offered her brother a slow nod, obviously letting him know he could expect payback for his comments. Jack couldn't help but smile at the affectionate sibling interaction. A part of him was envious at their bond. Would he and Daniel have been like Lucy and Travis? He brushed the thought away.

Travis turned to Lucy. "I just got a call. Beau is loose. We're on lockdown."

Lucy released a breath. "Of course he is. Any sightings?"

"Not yet."

"Did you drive the Ute over, Trav?" Lucy asked.

"Yeah. It's parked behind out back, on the street."

"Mind if I borrow it to take Mr. Harris on a little tour?"

"No problem." He tossed her the keys.

"Ute?" Jack asked as he followed Lucy out the back door and down a gravel walk.

"Utility vehicle. Like if a Jeep and a golf cart had a child."

Jack smiled when he saw the black vehicle with the ranch logo emblazoned on the hood. "That's a fitting description," he said as he slid into the doorless passenger side.

"What was Travis talking about? Beau?"

"The boys' ranch mascot. Beau is literally an old goat. He's nearly blind, mostly hard of hearing, yet somehow, he manages to get out of his corral now and then."

"A goat?"

She nodded. "You better fasten your seat belt, Mr. Harris. Around here you never can tell what might be waiting down the road."

He stretched the seat belt across himself and connected it with a click. "Couldn't you call me Jack or Jackson? Mr. Harris seems a little formal."

Lucy shrugged. "That's fine. However, our children will be calling you Mr. Jack. Those are the rules."

"What about you?" he asked.

"What about me?" Lucy put a hand on the gearshift knob.

"What do they call you?"

"Miss Lucy works." She paused. "I mean for the kids. You may call me Lucy."

"Thanks, Lucy."

She shot him a sidelong glance.

"Can you tell me about the ranch?" he asked.

Lucy turned in her seat. "I'm sure you had us investigated. Exactly what is it that was left out of your report?"

"Your family's qualifications for running this operation."

"I'm an orphan." The words were a flat admission. "Obviously, my brother and sister, as well. We cycled through the foster care system until we were adopted out." She shrugged and started the Ute. "More than you probably care to know."

Jack paused. He understood and cared far more than Lucy Maxwell would ever know. When his brother died, he too had been orphaned. His mother had taken off and his father had checked out.

Aunt Meri had saved him. He needed to remember that. His aunt was the only reason he was giving Big Heart Ranch a second chance.

She steered the Ute toward the main ranch road. "I have a master's degree in business management from Spears College of Business Management. Travis majored in animal sciences and graduated from the Oklahoma State University College of Agriculture and Natural Sciences. Emma also attended OSU and is a licensed social worker with a master's degree."

"How did three orphans manage that?"

Lucy's head jerked back at his question and she inhaled sharply. Slowing the Ute to a stop, she shifted into Neutral to look at him. "Excuse me?"

He raised a palm. "Don't read something into my words I didn't intend. My questions are simply part of my due diligence."

Silence reigned for moments, as she stared straight out the windshield of the Ute. When she turned to him once again, her eyes were shuttered.

"In addition to scholarships, we sold snake oil on Saturdays to fund our education."

Jack met her gaze. She didn't give him time to respond.

"As I stated, we were in the foster care system for several years. A cousin of our mother tracked us down and adopted all of us. I was ten, Travis was eight, Emma five. At the time, we were living in separate homes with monthly visitation."

"Separated from your siblings? That had to be tough."

"I'm not looking for pity."

"I wasn't offering pity."

She nodded and said nothing for several moments.

"You inherited the ranch?" Jack asked.

"Yes. Our property is bordered by that hewn wood fence," Lucy said as she pointed to a fence in the distance.

Fingers tight on the wheel, she turned the Ute left and drove down a shady, tree-lined street. The redbuds and maples were thick with green foliage. The aroma of freshly mown grass rode on the slight breeze.

"These are the boys' homes." Lucy pointed to the redbrick, two-story, Colonial-style houses, each spaced two lots apart, occupying the right side of the street. The left side was fenced, and horses grazed in the pasture.

A group of helmeted cyclists rode by, all young girls with arms extended to offer enthusiastic waves. "Hi, Miss Lucy!" they called in unison.

Lucy raised a hand out the vehicle in greeting.

"Why aren't they in school?"

"It's summer, Mr.— Uh, Jack."

He turned to look at the pasture on the right. "Cattle? That seems ambitious."

"That's us, and why not? Travis has graduated from the OSU Master Cattleman Program. He's worked several area ranches over the years."

"He's an impressive guy."

"There's not a person on the ranch who isn't impressive. We function with a staff of qualified professionals and volunteers. We need and value everyone. I hope you'll note that when you review our funding."

Jack stared out the window as they passed horses nibbling on grass and clover, their tails swishing at flies in the summer heat. The ranch was beautiful, he'd give her that. A part of him longed to walk through the fields spread before him, like he had as a child, when he hadn't had any cares. He and Daniel would lie on their backs in his aunt's pasture, finding shapes in the fluffy clouds that slowly moved across the endless blue Oklahoma summer sky.

A drop of sweat rolled down the back of his shirt, bringing him back to reality. Jack shifted uncomfortably. "I'd forgotten about how hot it is here in July."

Lucy shrugged. "You'll get used to the weather. The nice thing about the Oklahoma humidity is that it makes everything grow. You should see our vegetable garden."

He turned to her and raised a brow. "Vegetable garden, as well?"

"Yes. I hope you're sensing a pattern." Lucy offered a proud smile. "We want to be as self-sustaining as possible. Growing things also gives our children an appreciation for everything the Lord provides. We don't ever want to take that for granted. The more we do for ourselves, the better stewards we can be of the financial blessings we receive."

Jack said nothing to the obvious jibe.

"Look over there. Through the trees," Lucy said. "Girls' ranch. You'll actually get a close-up of everything after you receive your chore assignment."

"Chore assignment?"

"Everyone at the ranch has chores."

Jack wrapped his mind around that bit of information and stared out the window. A moment later, Lucy hit the brakes hard. He lurched forward, thrusting a hand to the dashboard in protection as the vehicle suddenly came to a complete halt.

"Sorry," Lucy said. "Are you okay?"

"Yeah. Is this how you usually drive?"

"No. Look to your right."

Jack glanced out in the field. "More cows."

"Our missing goat is out there, too."

"What's that?" Jack pointed to a black hen that strutted along the right side of the road, her black tail feathers raised regally.

"Mrs. Carmody got out, too!"

"You lose animals often here at the ranch?"

"They must have heard you were coming. However, to be fair, Beau and Mrs. Carmody escape every chance they can."

"You name all your chickens?"

"We do. Come on, let's go get her."

Jack blinked. "What?"

"You walk toward her and I'll circle around behind."

"What about the goat?"

"He'll be easy. I told you he's got vision and hearing issues. As for Mrs. C., she's an old hen and doesn't move very fast. She'll be easy, too."

"How'd she get out anyhow?"

"I don't know. Let's catch her and then I'll be sure to ask."

Jack frowned at the response and stepped from the Ute.

"You walk toward her and I'll circle behind."

"Are you sure this is going to work?"

"No. I'm not sure of anything," she said with a grin. "If you have a better idea, I'm open to suggestions."

Jack moved toward the chicken.

"Flap your arms," Lucy said.

"Flap my arms?"

"Why?"

"Let her know you're friendly." She cocked her head. "You don't have any medical conditions that preclude you from flapping, do you?"

"No. But I try not to look like a fool on principle."

Lucy began to laugh.

He paused for a moment at the sound of her laughter bubbling over. Then, despite his better judgment, Jack tucked his hands under and moved his arms up and down.

The chicken wasn't impressed. She slowly scratched at the ground and then began to run toward him on wobbly claws. "Why is she charging me?" Jack yelled.

"This is Mrs. Carmody and she doesn't follow the fowl rules."

Jack's eyes rounded when the bird attempted liftoff, her black wings flapping furiously. *Could chickens fly?*

This one managed a small liftoff before landing on her backside. Regrouping, the beady-eyed bird targeted him, one step at a time. Suddenly she picked up speed.

"Old and not very fast, huh? That bird is going to attack!"

Jack turned and ran, straight into a pile of something soft and wet. "Oomph!" His feet slid out from under him, and he landed on his back in the sweet grass.

"Good thing that grass hasn't been mowed yet," Lucy observed.

He opened his eyes. Mrs. Carmody was tucked neatly against Lucy, who stroked her feathers with her other hand. The chicken squawked and fussed for a moment, but Lucy held firm.

He had to give the ranch director credit; she'd grabbed the bird and was now doing an admirable job of trying not to laugh.

"Yeah, good thing," he returned as a black feather danced through the air and landed on him.

"Why did she run at me?" Jack asked.

"She was running to you. Big difference. I think she mistook you for Travis. You're both about the same size and coloring. Travis always brings Mrs. Carmody treats."

"So you're saying that I ran for nothing."

She glanced away, lips twitching. "Um, yes."

"And the flapping?"

"To get you into the moment."

Lucy held out a hand, and he grasped her palm, heaving himself to a standing position. Their eyes met and he froze for a moment, lost in her gaze. Then he glanced down at his once spotless shoes, lifting one and then the other to inspect the soles. A pungent odor drifted to his nose and he cringed. "Manure? Is that what I slipped on?"

She nodded and sniffed the air. "Horse, I'd say. Fresh."

"Do you know how much these shoes cost?" Jack rubbed his feet back and forth on the long blades of grass.

"My guess is enough to feed one of our kids for a year."

Jack only grumbled in response, and then he stopped what he was doing and stared at Lucy.

"What?" she asked.

"Could you have caught Mrs. Carmody on your own?"

"Probably." She said the word slowly.

"That's what I thought. So you were having fun with the city guy."

"I'd like to think of it as breaking the ice. You and I have a whole summer to work together. We need to get along. Besides, if it's any consolation, you passed chicken flapping with an A plus."

Jack couldn't help himself. He started laughing, and when he stopped, his gaze met Lucy's.

Her lips parted sweetly, and he realized they had at least reached détente. In that moment he became aware that his obligation to remain objective while he investigated the ranch for the Brisbane Foundation would be compromised every time Lucy smiled at him.

"What about your goat?" he asked.

"You hold Mrs. Carmody and I'll go grab Beau."

He stepped back and held up his hands. "Ah, no thank you. Why don't I get the goat?"

"You're okay with that?"

"I'm okay with pretty much anything if it means not holding a chicken."

This time Lucy laughed as well, and her eyes were bright with amusement. "You know that chickens are on your chore list, right?"

"Not seriously?"

She nodded.

"So, how do I get Beau?"

"He's docile. Gently grasp the rope around his neck and lead him to the Ute."

"What about the cows?"

"Nary a bull in sight. You'll be fine."

Jack started across the field. He grimaced and shook his head as he skirted around a cow patty. Day one on Big Heart Ranch, and already he'd gotten up close and personal with a chicken and was about to bring home a lost goat.

Yeah, it was going to be an interesting summer.

# Chapter Three

Jack checked his watch as he tugged his shirttail free from his jeans. He'd made it through day one and would be off duty soon. All he had to do was get his final chore assignment of the day completed. Then he'd be on his way to T-town, a little shopping and a nice steak. Free until the alarm sounded tomorrow at 5:00 a.m.

He pulled the paper Lucy had given him from his pocket and checked the dates. No chicken assignment until after the trail ride and camping trip were complete. If things went in his favor, Mrs. Carmody would release all the birds before then. He'd even pay the bird to stage a coop-break.

For a moment, he simply smiled, thinking about the whole chicken incident. Lately, women had been getting one over on him left and right. Feathered females included.

At least the goat had cooperated.

He shook his head and turned the paper in his hand over. Stables, straight ahead. Or equestrian center, as Lucy Maxwell called the building. He'd been assigned his own horse. That thought alone made him smile.

It had been a long time since he'd been responsible for a horse. Twenty-five years ago, Aunt

Meredith's horses had been his saving grace. His aunt worked him so hard the summer Daniel died that he didn't have time to blame himself for his little brother's death. He'd mucked stalls, fed and exercised a stable full of horses from sunrise until bedtime. Then he fell into a hard sleep, too exhausted for the nightmares.

There was no denying the thrum of excitement that accompanied Jack as he entered the equestrian building. Except for the soft whinny of horses, it was quiet.

Jack smiled. He'd forgotten how good quiet was. The lights were on as he took his time walking down the center of the stables, his left hand reaching out to touch the gates of each stall he passed, like he was a kid again. He let the smells of horse sweat and hay nudge his memories while he searched for the sorrel mare he was about to groom.

Spotless. The boys' ranch stables were spotless, no strong urine odors to indicate the stalls were anything but clean. A chalkboard on the outside of the very last stall on the left had "Grace" printed in white chalk in a childish scrawl. He looked around and found the tack room, situated next to an office, whose door was shut, lights off. The sign on the door read Tripp Walker, Manager.

The familiar scent of new leather drifted to Jack's nostrils as he entered the tack room and grabbed supplies. He juggled a currycomb and soft brush in the air and caught them easily. His steps were light as he opened the latch to Grace's stall.

Jack Harris, in a barn. No one would believe it if they could see him now. He didn't believe it himself.

The mare shifted and raised her tail. Jack sidestepped, though not fast enough to avoid stepping in steaming and aromatic horse patties. He grimaced and held his breath. Twice in one day.

His life as an attorney was filled with horse patties, but today was a record.

Nope, no one would ever believe this, either.

"Grace," he told the mare. "I thought we were going to be friends. This is no way to treat a guy on our first date."

The horse merely nickered in response.

Jack grabbed a pitchfork and buried the foul evidence in fresh wood chips that he moved to the corner of the stall, before pulling the currycomb and a brush from his back pocket. He ran his open palm slowly along the coarse coat of reddish-gold of the animal's flank to prepare her for the session, and then gently began to comb the horse.

"There you go, Grace. Feels good, doesn't it?" he soothed. "When we're done, I have a nice carrot for you." With two fingers, he massaged the animal's wide forehead until she relaxed.

Jack stuck his nose right into her neck and rubbed the mare's ears as he inhaled. Yeah, this was the real perfume of summer. The sweet, subtle sweat of horse hair. Pleasant memories of days with Aunt Meri tumbled through his mind.

Jack continued to brush the mare, one hand on the brush, the other on the animal's silky-soft back. The tension he didn't realize he held evaporated into the small space.

"You're doing it wrong," a small voice whispered.

Jack paused, and Grace's ears perked at the voice. A quick glance around the stall revealed nothing and no one. Jack continued brushing.

"Circles. You gotta do it in circles."

He opened the metal gate and took a quick peek down the main walkway and then into the stalls on either side of Grace's. Both stalls had horses, but they appeared to be the nontalking variety. "Where are you?" Jack asked.

"Up here."

Jack frowned before glancing straight up. To the right was a hay storage shelf where a little boy, no more than five or six, smiled down at him with a toothy grin. His upper front teeth were absent.

"Are you supposed to be up there?" Jack asked.

The urchin with a dirty face and hair the color of straw shrugged. "No one cares."

"I bet Miss Lucy cares," Jack said.

The kid wore jeans and battered red sneakers, the laces untied. Scooting to the edge, he dangled his legs. The movement knocked bits of straw into the air. Hay and dust danced on their way to the ground. Some landed on Jack and Grace.

"Kid, you're messing up my work here."

"Sorry." Which came out as *thorry* due to the missing teeth.

"What's your name?"

"Dub Lewis."

"Your name is Dub?"

"Uh-huh. What's your name?"

"Jackson Harris."

Dub screwed up his face and giggled. "What kind of name is that?"

Jack smiled. No filter. His brother had been the same way. Said whatever came to mind, whenever it came to mind.

He chuckled. "Touché, kid."

"You want me to show you how to do that?" Dub asked.

"Do what?" Jack looked up again, and then down at his hand paused on the horse's flank. "*This?* I've been grooming horses since I was your age."

That might be a slight exaggeration, but it silenced the kid, who was obviously five going on thirty.

Jack pulled out the soft brush and began to clean the area the currycomb had covered.

Silence reigned until Jack began to pick Grace's hooves.

"Are you supposed to be here?" Dub asked.

"Yes." Jack cocked his head. "I think the real question is, are you supposed to be here?"

"I gots permission."

"So you said."

"Grace is my horse. Leo said. And he's going to teach me to ride Grace."

"Who's Leo?"

"Leo. You know. Leo."

"Actually, I don't know. But I can ask Miss Lucy about it if you want me to."

Again with the shrug of the bony shoulders. Jack stared at the kid for a moment. He couldn't remember the last time he'd been around a child. Normally, he avoided them. Too much responsibility and too many memories.

Jack moved on to the next hoof, battling an urge to check and see if the kid was giving him an approving scrutiny. *Hoof picking, Harris.* He reminded himself. *You've got this covered.*

"Aren't you going to the meeting?" Dub asked.

"Meeting?"

"Uh-huh. Right before dinner."

"Maybe *you* have a meeting, but I don't think I do."

"The meeting's for everyone," the kid insisted.

Jack vaguely recalled a meeting listed on his schedule for today that he planned to miss.

"I don't think I need to attend."

"Everyone does. Miss Lucy said it's for the trail ride."

"You're kind of young for a trail ride. How old are you, anyhow?"

"I'm five and I'm going." He gave an adamant shake of his blond head. "Yeth, I am."

"Okay. Fine."

He grabbed the tools and closed the stall behind him before offering her the carrot. "Good girl, Grace."

The mare snorted and accepted her treat.

"She likes carrots best."

Jack nodded. "She sure does. So, Dub Lewis, I don't suppose you know where this meeting is?" Jack asked.

"Uh-huh. The chow hall. Want me to show you?"

"I'll find it." Jack put the tools away and looked up at the little boy. "How are you going to get down?"

"Ladder."

"Be careful, kid, would you?" he said as he finished with Grace and closed the stall gate behind him.

A moment later Dub Lewis appeared at his side. The kid seemed small for his age. But what did Jack know about kids? Nothing. And he planned to keep it that way.

"Why aren't you wearing boots?" Jack asked. "It's dangerous to be in the stables without boots on."

"I wasn't in the stall," he lisped.

"Sure you were."

Dub shook his head. "I was in the loft. You don't need boots in the loft."

Jack opened his mouth and closed it again. What was he doing? He was arguing with a five-year-old, that was what. Once again, the kid reminded him of Daniel. Same forthright attitude and stubborn streak.

"I'm watching Grace," Dub said. "We're friends."

"Oh, yeah?"

Dub nodded, and his short legs did double time in an effort to keep up with Jack, who continued to put the supplies away in the tack room.

"Yeth," he said. "Sometimes I get to ride Grace, but I gotta wear a helmet."

"They let you run around the ranch all by yourself, too?" Jack asked.

"I'm not running around. 'Sides, I told you. I gots permission."

"Gots, huh?" Jack resisted the urge to smile. This was serious stuff. A five-year-old had no business running around without supervision. He knew only too well what could happen. Jack swallowed hard, finding himself getting tense and annoyed all over again.

Dub tugged on Jack's shirttail. "Come on, Mr. Jackson, or we'll be late."

He regarded the pint-size kid at his side. "I'm Jack. Mr. Jack."

And what was with this "we" stuff?

"Hurry, Mr. Jack!"

"How do you know we'll be late?" he asked Dub. "You don't have a watch on."

"I could see from the window up there. Everybody's walking to the chow hall."

"Okay, fine. Show me the way."

Dub was right. There were a lot of kids walking toward the training building. Now that he thought of it, he recalled a cafeteria in that building.

A few adults were up ahead, but it was mostly kids. Lots of kids. Boys of different ages laughed and talked as they headed to the meeting.

Somehow the whole kids at the ranch thing had slipped Jack's mind. He hadn't connected the dots. Or he had, and then blocked it out. Jack swiped a hand over his face and swallowed, willing his heart rate to slow down.

It didn't matter—he wasn't here for kids. He was here as a ranch hand. He'd do chickens and goats, and anything else the director lady threw at him. But kids were definitely not part of his repertoire. Not now and not in the future.

He stole a glance at the boy beside him. A prickle of apprehension raced over him, and he realized that he needed to make his no-kids policy completely clear to Lucy Maxwell.

And to Dub Lewis.

Lucy blinked.

What was Jack Harris doing with Dub Lewis?

At well over six feet, he had to lean over every now and again to catch what the small child was saying. Dub seemed to be talking nonstop, skipping at intervals to keep up with Jack's long strides. Jack's dark head was next to Dub's blond one. Lucy's heart gave a little swoon at the picture they made. But Jack wasn't smiling. The attorney limped as he walked—a sure sign those fancy shoes were causing him considerable discomfort.

"Did you get all moved in?" she murmured as he approached.

"I did," he said with a curt nod.

"You spoke with your aunt?"

"My aunt." He chuckled. "Aunt Meri cleverly left town to spend a few days with a friend."

Lucy smiled and glanced from Jack to the little boy at his side. "I see you met Dub."

"Met? He seems to have permanently attached himself to my shadow. I have a few questions for you," Jack said, his words for her ears only.

Lucy knelt down next to Dub. "Hey, Dub, why don't you go ahead and find a seat inside?"

Dub glanced at the box of camping supplies at her side. "Don't I need those, too?"

"Miss Lorna picked yours up for you."

"Okay. Are we still going for ice cream?" He searched her face hopefully. "With my sissies?"

"What did I tell you?" she returned.

"You said that you'd pick us up tonight after dinner."

"That's correct, and I always keep my promises." Relief now shone in Dub's eyes.

"Now go ahead and find a seat inside, please."

"Okay." He turned to Jack. "I'll save you a seat, Mr. Jack."

"Uh, thanks, kid."

Lucy's gaze followed Dub as he raced into the open door of the building.

"What's his story?" Jack asked.

She turned to face him. "What do you mean?"

"Seems like he should be in an orphanage so he can be adopted. Your facility isn't licensed for adoption."

"You really did your research," Lucy said with a grudging smile. "Once again, I'm impressed."

"Don't be. I'm sure I'll annoy you again very soon."

"Dub is here as a favor to the court."

"Why?"

"He's one of three."

"Three?"

"Yes. Triplets."

Jack's eyes rounded. "There are three of him? Where are his brothers?"

"Sisters. Ann and Eva. They're at the girls' ranch."

"How's that work?"

"Normally different-sex siblings have visitation weekly. We provide extra family time together for the triplets."

"So why are they here?"

"You understand this falls under the medical confidentiality agreement you signed. We expect that of all staff members."

"I'm an attorney. I'm accustomed to keeping my mouth shut."

Though she sorely itched to spout the hearty comeback on the tip of her tongue, Lucy recognized that she was supposed to be making nice with the man, so she bit her tongue instead.

"Finding foster parents willing to take triplets isn't easy. Dub was in a separate foster home from his sisters and he became very depressed. In fact, Dub has been in three different foster homes already this year. He ran away from all of them."

"Why? Why does he run away? Do they treat him poorly?"

"Not at all. Dub simply feels obligated to take care of his sisters. That's his burden. So he leaves to find them."

"That's a heavy load for a five-year-old."

"I know." And she did, far more than anyone would ever understand. It had been her job, like Dub's, to keep track of Emma and Travis when the three of them were in foster care.

"How far does the little man get?" Jack asked.

"Oh, you'd be surprised." She released a sigh. "Our Dub is very resourceful."

"Now he's here."

"Yes. Dub and his sisters are here for the summer at least, to keep them together."

"How long have they been in the system?"

"A year. They were removed from their home due to neglect and abandonment. Poor kids were left alone quite a bit, and expected to fend for themselves by the only custodial parent."

Jack grimaced. "Mother?"

"Yes."

"And the father?"

"Unknown."

He shook his head and glanced at the building Dub had gone into. Lucy blinked at the emotion Harris wore on his face. It was the first emotion she'd seen him express for anyone besides his aunt.

"That's a tough break for a kid," he muttered.

She nodded. "Another reason they're here is to see if Dub flourishes when his only responsibility is being a kid. At the ranch, he knows his sisters are being taken care of. A few times he's randomly asked to see them in the middle of the day. It was as if he needed to be sure they were safe. We complied, and he was able to stop worrying. Dub trusts us to keep our word."

"How is his being here going to help with the adoption process?"

"We're actively trying to find Dub a home, and we've agreed to facilitate any potential foster or adoptive parents who are interested in all three children."

Jack offered a short nod, annoyance still evident on his face. "The kid was in the stables." He shot her an accusatory look. "Alone. No supervision."

"Dub always asks permission, and he knows that he's not allowed in the stalls."

"That's not the same as supervision."

"Dub understands the rules."

"So he kept telling me. Yet seeing him in the loft, a good fifteen feet above the ground, I was not reassured."

She stepped closer and lowered her voice. "We have security cameras and microphones in the stables. Off-site security is monitoring most of this ranch, except for the pastures. Soon we'll have cameras out there, as well." It was her turn to look him in the eye. "If our budget is approved."

"Cameras don't take the place of adults supervising kids. He was in the loft. Is that allowed?"

"That would be a loophole in our agreement. Kids tend to find those. You're an attorney— surely you understand loopholes."

"A loophole?"

"Yes. He wasn't technically in the stall. But I appreciate the heads-up. I will discuss that with Dub." She paused. "I do want you to know that we've been operating for five years, and no child has ever been seriously injured."

"Trust me. It only takes one second for things

to spiral out of control. And in that moment, the rest of your life is changed. *Forever.*"

She stared at him, assessing the rigid posture, the hands shoved into his pockets. More emotion. Where was it all coming from? Jack Harris was hiding a painful secret, of that she was certain. Her words were slow and measured when she responded. "Are you asking for Dub as your buddy for the summer? Is that what this is all about?"

"What?" His head jerked back and his hands came up, palms out. "No. I don't even know anything about buddies."

"You have to pick someone. Why not Dub? He certainly seems to have attached himself to you."

Jack lifted his palms again and stepped back. "Whoa. I have zero experience with kids."

"Weren't you a kid?"

"That was a very limited engagement. It ended when I was nine."

"What?"

He grimaced. "Trust me. I am not the man to be in charge of a kid."

Lucy opened her mouth to answer and then closed it again. Somehow she knew that he was telling the truth, and his words troubled her. What had happened to Jack Harris to make him so nervous at the thought of being with a child?

She pushed back her bangs. "All you have to do is accompany him on the various summer activities. Be his designated adult. Give him your undivided attention and unconditional love."

Was she imagining things, or did Jack pale as she spoke?

He wiped his palms on his jeans. "How long does this buddy thing last?" he asked.

"Until the end of summer."

"You expect me to babysit Dub for six weeks?"

"Please lower your voice." Again, Lucy glanced around. "We don't call our ministry at the ranch babysitting. We're sharing and caring."

"Sharing and caring." Jack ran a hand over his face and rubbed the small scar on the bridge of his nose with his index finger.

Lucy stepped closer to Jack as a few volunteers and children walked past her and into the chow hall. "Are you all right?" she asked quietly.

He skirted the question with one of his own. "What if he doesn't trust me? You said he already has issues."

"Jack, it's obvious Dub's already bonded with you."

"What makes you think that?" The lawyer's eyes narrowed.

"Dub Lewis doesn't follow everyone around. Besides, part of the connection is that horse. Grace. You're assigned to Grace and he loves that mare."

Jack knit his brows together. "Dub says Grace is Leo's horse."

"No, Leo was just in charge of cleaning the stalls. Leo is actually gone."

"What happened?"

"He needed a raise that we were unable to provide, given our current, uh…economic situation. It's unfortunate because Leo did the work of several employees."

This time Jack's eyes popped wide. "Does that make me the new Leo?"

"In a manner of speaking, yes, I guess so. However, whether you buddy with Dub or not is your decision." She shrugged. "You will be assigned a buddy."

"What part of 'I don't want a buddy' don't you get?"

Lucy grit her teeth and tamped back a surge of irritation. "What did you think you were going to do at the ranch? Ride a horse and play cowboy?"

"I didn't *think* at all. You insisted I see what the ranch was all about."

"Yes. That's because you were about to pull the rug out from under us. We're privately funded. Meredith believes in what we do here. I'm hoping you will, too. We need that funding."

"I'm not here to take care of kids." His words were flat.

Jack Harris had returned to his hard-hearted self. That was too bad, because she was starting to sort of almost like him.

"Look, Jack, this ranch is the real thing. You are expected to fully participate."

"What does that mean?"

"Not only will you have a buddy assignment, but starting tomorrow you'll start your full chore list and participate in all required activities, including the trail ride and campout."

"But…"

"Is there a problem? You certainly were quick to dismiss us to your aunt. Now that you actually have to get your hands dirty, you're having second thoughts? I'm happy to call Meredith."

"No. There's no need to bother my aunt."

Lucy glanced at her watch. "I have to start this meeting soon."

She reached down and grabbed a pup tent and sleeping bag from the boxes next to her and shoved them at Jack.

He staggered backward in surprise.

"If you lose them, you buy them." When she moved toward the doors Lucy was surprised to discover Jack matching his steps to her own.

"Tell me about the trail ride."

Lucy kept walking, stopping only to open the glass doors for him since his arms were full. "It's exactly that. The junior high and high school kids participate each year for three days and two nights. This first session is the boys' ranch."

Jack repositioned the tent pack and the sleeping bag in his arms. "Three days in the saddle?" he asked.

"No, we only ride horses there and back. It's a camping experience. We take the chuck wagon and live outside with no electronics."

"No cell phones?"

"None. Not that it really matters. Cell reception is nil where we're headed."

"You're telling me that they actually like doing this?"

"The staff and the children look forward to this particular event every year."

"Really?" His eyes narrowed as he considered her words.

"You know people pay a small fortune for this kind of outdoor experience. We offer it to our kids free of charge."

Lucy looked at him. The man was privileged. Could he possibly understand? "You have no idea what an opportunity this is for kids who have been forgotten in foster care or suffered the emotional abyss of abusive situations." She couldn't help herself as the words began to tumble from her mouth unfiltered. "Please don't discount this event until you've experienced the trail ride for yourself."

For once Jack Harris was silent.

"Are you up for the challenge?" she asked.

"Do I have a choice?"

"Everyone has a choice. You and I need to put

our differences aside for the summer because the children of Big Heart Ranch come first."

When he didn't answer, she took a deep breath. "Can we work together for six weeks or not, Jack?"

"I guess we'll have to try, won't we?"

"It's all up to you, Jack." Lucy nodded toward the back of the chow hall, where Dub Lewis waved his stubby arms. "Your buddy has your seat saved."

Jack released a resigned sigh as his gaze followed hers. When he started across the room, a limp was still evident.

"Oh, and Jack?"

He turned, brows raised. "Yeah?"

"Moleskin."

"Excuse me?"

"Try moleskin and a little triple antibiotic ointment for those blisters."

His gaze shot to his shoes, and he immediately stopped limping. "I don't have blisters. The only thing rubbing me the wrong way is this ranch."

Lucy clutched her clipboard to her chest as she inhaled slowly, counting to ten while willing herself not to respond. Keeping her mouth shut every time Jack Harris pushed her buttons might very well prove to be the most difficult challenge of the next six weeks.

# Chapter Four

They'd been on the trail almost three hours. Jack pushed his ball cap to the back of his head and pulled off his sunglasses to peer at the clear azure sky. The July sun's merciless rays mocked him.

He shifted in the saddle, to no avail. His backside still ached and his T-shirt clung to his damp skin. Who went on a trail ride in one-hundred-degree weather? The humidity made the air so thick that he could taste it each time he opened his mouth.

From the bits of conversation that drifted back from the front of the line of horses and riders, everyone else seemed to be in good spirits.

Yeah, this was definitely an acquired taste. Jack took a swig of water and positioned Grace so the horse trotted behind the chuck wagon.

Covered with waterproof canvas and led by two horses, the wagon looked like an old-fashioned movie prop. More important was that it was large enough to hide Jack from inquisitive eyes as he peered at his banned electronic device.

Grace offered a snuffle and snort, shaking her head back and forth as though in warning when he slid his phone from his pocket and checked for reception.

No signal.

*Again.*

He had to admit that it irked him that so far Lucy Maxwell had been right about everything. From his blisters to the cell reception.

At the back of the wagon, the right canvas flap flew open and Dub Lewis stuck his head out, a huge toothless grin on his freckled face.

"Hi, Mr. Jack!" he called.

"Hey, isn't that dangerous?" Jack returned. "You might fall out of there."

"I have a seat belt on."

"Yeah, well, be careful."

"I will."

"You better," Jack grumbled.

The smile on Dub's face widened as he continued to chatter. "You've got Grace. Can I ride her?"

"Maybe." Jack offered a begrudging smile at the kid's enthusiasm.

"Did you know that we're having carrot cake later?"

"Oh, yeah?"

Dub nodded, eyes rounding.

"It's Auggie's birthday," a familiar female voice said from behind Jack. The soft thud of horse hooves and the jingle of tack told him she was approaching on his right.

*Lucy.* Jack slid his phone back into the pocket of his jeans.

"Who is Auggie?" he asked, turning slightly in the saddle.

Seated confidently on a black mare, in Levi's and her red ranch logo T-shirt, Lucy was all smiles today. She held the reins with soft chamois gloves and nodded up ahead, where a dozen or so boys wearing riding helmets bounced gently in the saddle, along with the rhythmic motion of their horses.

"See the tall boy with the black helmet? The one on the chestnut mare? Near the end?"

Jack nodded.

"This is the first time in his life he's ever celebrated his birthday."

"What do you mean?" Jack said, hoping her words weren't literal.

"Exactly that."

"How is that possible?"

"Neglect and abuse situations. We see it more often than you want to know." She shrugged. "But today he's already had a birthday breakfast and opened presents before we started the trail ride. Plus, our cook for the trip has brought along a cake and a few surprises."

"That doesn't sound like roughing it to me."

"Aw, come on, Jack. Lighten up, would you? It's a birthday. We consider them part of creating family traditions for our kids."

"Traditions?" he muttered.

"Sure. Things you probably take for granted, like holidays and special celebrations, and yes, birthdays."

"What about you?" he asked.

"What about me?"

"Did you have traditions growing up?"

"Things became a little blurry once we lost my parents." Lucy pulled a foot from the stirrup, showing off one of the hand-tooled red leather boots. "See these boots?"

"Yeah, they're hard to miss."

"I asked for red boots for my birthday one year when I was a foster. I wanted them so badly. Of course, I didn't get them. But the biological daughter of my foster parents did. For no reason. It wasn't her birthday, and she hadn't asked for them."

Lucy smiled and glanced down at the boot with pride, carefully placing her foot back in the stirrup. "I bought myself these boots. Every single time I put them on I am reminded of why I do this job. It's because every kid deserves red boots for their birthday."

Jack did his best to keep what he was feeling from showing on his face. Lucy Maxwell wouldn't want to be pitied. He flashed back to his last birthday with his brother. Blowing out candles and opening presents.

Bicycles. They'd both wanted bicycles, as badly as Lucy had wanted her boots.

He swallowed hard. They'd gotten them, too. Daniel's bicycle was still somewhere at his aunt's house. Before he could dwell on the thought, the flap of the wagon popped open once more.

Dub stuck his head outside to flash them a smile and disappeared again.

"Is that safe?" Jack gestured toward the wagon. "Seems to me he could go bouncing around."

"The wagon was specially made for the ranch, and not only does it have an authentic flour cupboard and a cooking shelf on the outside, but it was also fitted with four seats that have full seat belts. It's very safe."

"Once again, I'm impressed. Where did it come from?"

"Donated by a local carpenter."

"Is Dub the only one riding inside of there?"

"Yes. He's the only child under ten on this trip."

"Was that in my honor? Because he's my buddy?"

"You flatter yourself." She tipped the brim of her straw Stetson lower against the sun. "Dub's entire ranch family is on the trail ride. House parents included. We thought it would be good for him to join us."

"There are lots of things for a little kid to get into on a camping trip. Accidents happen when you least expect them."

"Sounds like you have firsthand knowledge. Care to share?"

Jack stiffened. No, he wasn't ready to bare his soul to a woman he hardly knew. A woman he was supposed to be investigating. He shook his head and glanced away.

"He knows the rules, Jack. And he's going to stick to you like…well, you know."

"Terrific. He's not going to be in my tent, is he?"

"No, he's sleeping with two of his ranch brothers."

"What exactly is the point of this trip?"

"The point?" She released a breath and stared at him, hands on the saddle horn. "Does everything have to have a point?"

"Yes. You're utilizing plenty of ranch resources. Donated resources. I'm trying to understand the value."

"Jack, it's about planting seeds. Sometimes you can't see the harvest. You have to trust that by doing what you are called to do, what this ranch is called to do, the harvest will be there."

"How does the trail ride fit into your harvest?"

"First and foremost, this is all about fun. Think like a kid for a minute, instead of an attorney. These are children who are accustomed to going to bed on broken glass, emotionally. In their former life, they went to sleep uncertain what tomorrow would bring. We promise them that they don't have to think about tomorrow. They can simply be kids." Her chocolate eyes continued to pin him.

Against his better judgment, he paused to consider her words. *Just be a kid?* He hadn't been "just a kid" since that summer so long ago. Jack raised his head and met her gaze. Words refused to come.

Lucy sighed when he didn't respond. "Ah, Jack, you don't understand." The words were laced with deep regret.

Jack swallowed hard. He did understand. Far more than Lucy would ever realize.

Up ahead, a horse whinnied and laughter broke out, soon turning into raised voices. The raised voices changed into shouts of anger. The unexpected stop of the chuck wagon caused the rear of the entourage to stop. Like dominos falling over, horses were forced to sidestep with the sudden halt. Their protesting whinnies filled the morning air.

"Excuse me," Lucy said. She picked up her reins and nosed her horse off the well-worn path, through the wild grass and around the wagon.

"Hit him again, Matt," a voice rang out.

Jack pulled Grace's reins to the left in an attempt to figure out what was going on. And then he saw what everyone was looking at. Two teenage boys were entangled on the ground, rolling from the dusty trail to the grass with fists flying. Jack ushered Grace ahead and into a trot.

"Stop this, right now!" Lucy yelled. She slid from her horse as two men pulled the boys apart. Good-size teenagers, they struggled to get free and reach the object of their wrath: each other.

The riders up ahead had stopped and turned in their saddles to see what was going on behind them.

The boys stumbled around, kicking up dust with their boots, stretching from the hands that held them, fists flailing in the air as they continued to struggle.

Lucy stepped into the space between the boys.

"Not a good idea," Jack muttered. "Never get between two opposing forces."

One of the boys broke loose. When he shot forward to grab his opponent, his shoulder knocked into Lucy.

"Lucy!" Jack shouted, realizing the warning was coming much too late.

Down went the ranch director.

"You hit Miss Lucy," a voice accused.

Gasps, followed by a hushed silence, filled the air as Jack leaped from Grace to the ground beside Lucy's limp body.

A stunned Lucy blinked when Jack wrapped his arm around her shoulders and helped her to a seated position. Then the dark lashes fluttered closed, resting against her too pale cheeks.

Jack's hands trembled as he held her, and emotion slammed into him as hard as the protective urge that rose when he tucked her slim frame against his chest. From deep inside, his brain furiously balked at the unexpected tenderness so suddenly roused. But for the first time in a long time, he ignored that analytical voice. Right now, all that mattered was that Lucy was okay.

Around him, denim-clad legs crowded closer as riders hovered.

"Move back!" Jack thundered. His words were laced with an unspoken threat, and he didn't care who heard it.

"Go get Rue," someone urged.

Jack assessed the too still woman, fear and adrenaline kicking his heart rate into overdrive.

"Everyone, please stand back. We need a little air," a female commanded a few minutes later. A tank of a middle-aged woman with gray curls, wearing a faded and wrinkled version of the red ranch T-shirt and a straw Stetson with a hole in the brim, slid to the ground next to Jack. With a brief glance in his direction, she opened a battered leather medical bag. "What happened?"

"She got in the way of an argument," Jack said. He looked up at the crowd surrounding them. The guilty teenager swallowed hard, his face pale and filled with shame.

"Matt and Abel." The woman glanced up at the boys. "Seriously? Again?"

"I take it they don't like each other," Jack said.

"No, they love each other. They're biological brothers. That's the problem."

"Are you a doctor?" he asked when she tossed him a pair of surgical gloves and slipped on another pair herself.

"Correct. Dr. Rue Butterfield." She nodded. "Consider yourself deputized as my assistant."

"Code of the West?" he asked, as he picked up the bright blue gloves.

"Yep." She gently checked Lucy's pulse. "Lucy? Honey, can you hear me?"

Lucy moaned, her eyes opening and then closing again. "What happened?" She reached a hand to touch the back of her head. "Ouch."

"Sit still and lean forward," Rue said when she tried to stand. "Let me check your head."

Rue pointed to a gauze pad. "Can you tear that open for me?"

"She's bleeding?"

"A small cut at the back of her head, along with a small lump."

Jack tore open the package and handed Rue the gauze pad.

"So you're Leo's replacement."

"Am I?" He met her no-nonsense dark eyes.

"Jack Harris, right?"

"Yeah. How'd you know?"

"Word travels faster than a sneeze through a screen door around here. We heard Meredith Brisbane's stuck-up lawyer nephew stopped the funding to the ranch."

"Rue," Lucy whispered, her voice shaky.

The woman continued despite Lucy's protest. "I heard that there was a volunteer here for the summer taking his place." Her gaze was intent as she assessed him. "You have your work cut out for you, Jack. Leo did the job of two men."

"I heard it was three," he returned.

Rue laughed. "Probably true. Point being, he wouldn't have left if Lucy could match the pay he was offered elsewhere. It's too bad our director here is the one picking up the slack. I'd like to give that attorney holding up the money a piece of my mind."

"Rue. Please," Lucy said with a warning tone in her voice.

"A real jerk, huh?" Jack said.

"Yep. I'd like to see him walk a day in Lucy's shoes. Then he might understand."

"That sounds like a really good idea," Jack said with a smile. "Maybe we can arrange it."

Rue smiled back. "I like you, Jack." She pulled a penlight from her pocket and checked Lucy's pupils. "And I appreciate you stepping up to save the day. We need more men like you around Big Heart Ranch."

"Thanks, but perhaps you should hold your kind words until summer is over."

"I'm a good judge of character. I doubt you can

do anything that will change my opinion." She winked and turned to Lucy.

"Anything in particular hurt, Lucy?" Rue asked. "Besides the head."

"My dignity."

Rue pulled a stethoscope from her bag. "I'll take a quick listen and do a little palpation, honey. Just want to make sure you didn't break a rib or anything."

When she finished her evaluation, Rue pulled the stethoscope from her ears and nodded. "So far everything seems fine."

Lucy attempted to stand.

"No. Not just yet." She looked to Jack. "I'm going to go get ice. Keep an eye on her. She may have a concussion."

"Will do," he said.

"You're going to expel those boys who were fighting, right?" Jack asked once Rue was out of earshot.

"It was my fault. I got between them," Lucy said.

"Lucy, you were knocked down."

"It was an accident."

"I'm not so sure. You could easily file charges. Aggravated assault."

"Against who? Jack, the ranch is responsible for those boys. I'd be filing charges against my own ranch."

He paused, stymied by her logic. The woman was right again.

"Besides, they're brothers. Siblings fight. That's normal. Didn't you ever fight with a brother or sister?"

The question knocked him in the gut. Sure, he and Daniel had fought. And he'd give anything for another day to fight with him.

"Jack?" Lucy whispered. "Are you okay?"

"I don't have a sister," he said. "And my brother is dead."

She released a soft gasp. "I'm so sorry."

"Yeah. Me, too."

Once again, Lucy tried to stand.

"The doc said to sit still."

Rue returned with a plastic bag of ice in her hand. She looked between them. "Everything okay?"

"Your director is being stubborn."

Rue offered a hearty chuckle. "What else is new?"

"Hey, I'm right here," Lucy protested.

"So you are," Rue said. "Wrap a bandanna around the bag of ice and apply it to the lump on your head for as long as you can tolerate. Twenty minutes or so at a time. I'll be checking on you to be sure you don't have a concussion. Let me know if you're nauseated or dizzy."

"Shouldn't she go back to the ranch?" Jack asked.

"No!" Lucy interjected, sitting up straighter. "I'm fine. I'm also in charge this week."

Rue held up a hand. "Whoa, now, Lucy. Take it easy."

"I know the symptoms of a concussion. I'll be careful," Lucy said.

"I trust you will, and that you'll ride in the wagon with Dub," Rue said.

"My horse…"

"I'll handle your horse," Jack said. "How much farther is it anyhow?"

"About half a mile," Rue said. She turned to Lucy. "Do you want me to ride in the wagon with you?"

Lucy waved a hand. "Completely unnecessary."

"All right," the other woman said. "I'll check on you after we make camp."

"Thank you, Rue," Lucy said.

Jack echoed her words.

"No problem. It's my job. And thank you for your help, Jack." Rue offered him a broad smile.

"You certainly impressed General Butterfield," Lucy muttered as the doctor left. "That doesn't happen often."

"Did I?" He chuckled. "Why did you call her General?"

"Retired US Army. She volunteers full-time at the ranch."

"No kidding." He shook his head. "Could have

fooled me when she said she was a doctor. A general, too?"

"Not just a general. A two-star general. Judge nothing by its cover at Big Heart Ranch." Lucy put a palm on the ground and began to stand.

"Wait, let me help." He held out a hand.

Lucy grabbed her straw Stetson from the ground, dusted it off and jammed the crown on her head over her chin-length dark hair. With a sigh of resignation, she accepted Jack's outstretched palm. Her small hand fit neatly in his as he carefully assisted her to a standing position. "Feeling okay?"

She blinked and took a deep breath, but didn't meet his gaze. "I'm good," she murmured, slowly extricating her hand from his.

Lucy turned away from him in a quick movement and stumbled in the process. He reached for her arm.

"I've got it." Lucy nodded her thanks, before stepping away from his hand on her elbow. She dusted off her jeans and grimaced at the red dirt and grass stains marring her once pristine T-shirt.

Her eyes widened when he stepped toward her. "You've got stuff in your hair," Jack said. He reached forward, plucked a piece of leaf and twig from the dark tresses and placed them in her palm. "There's still…"

Nodding, she removed her hat and ran her

hands through the short cap of hair, ruffling the strands and releasing bits of grass and dirt.

"You got it," he said.

They stood facing each other, silent for a moment. "Thank you," Lucy murmured.

"No problem." When he pulled down the steps to the wagon and yanked back a flap of canvas, Dub instantly appeared.

The little man's jaw dropped for a moment, and then he screwed up his face. "Miss Lucy, are you okay?"

"She fell down," Jack said.

"We gots to pray for her, Mr. Jack."

"What?" Jack's head jerked back at the words.

"We gots to pray for her, right now."

"Dub, we can pray later," Lucy suggested.

"No. Miss Lucy, we learned in Bible study that you should pray now. Not later. Later doesn't always come."

"I, ah… I haven't prayed for anyone in a long time," Jack said.

"Don't worry. I'll show you how," Dub said. He took Lucy's and then Jack's hand in his small ones. "Now, close your eyes. I'll talk to God. Don't worry."

Jack swallowed hard and looked to Lucy, hoping for an escape route.

"Planting seeds," Lucy murmured.

Jack shook his head and then closed his eyes, swallowing hard as he recalled that he hadn't prayed in over twenty-five years. Not since that fateful day his brother died.

So today he would pray, because a five-year-old orphan had told him to, and because he realized that Dub was right. Despite his misgivings about Big Heart Ranch, Lucy Maxwell still deserved his prayers.

Jack opened his eyes and rested his gaze on Lucy, and his thoughts whispered softly, reminding him how right the woman felt in his arms. In that moment, he reluctantly admitted that maybe he needed prayer, too.

"So you're sort of a white-collar rebel. Aren't you?" Lucy asked as she approached Jack Harris.

"Is that a trick question?"

The light from the campfire silhouetted his strong profile as he stood in front of what was supposed to be his tent. It also illuminated the cell phone in his hand, and Lucy clucked her tongue in dismay.

"Everyone else set up their tents hours ago." She switched on the flashlight in her hand and shone the beam over the tarp and poles at his feet. "What are you doing?"

Jack casually eased his phone into the back pocket of his blue jeans, picked up a pole and fit it into another. "Is that a rhetorical question?"

She slowly shook her head. "You know, I would have never taken you for a rule breaker."

"Rule breaker?"

"You're using electronics."

"I'm trying to put a tent together, ideally before midnight."

He looked at his watch, an expensive electronic gadget that no doubt cost more than her car.

"Nice watch. Does it talk to your phone and your laptop, and monitor your heart rate and the size of your ego and all that good stuff?"

"Yeah. It does. Except for the ego part." He met her gaze and raised a hand. "I know what you're thinking, but in my defense, this tent did not come with instructions."

"That's because everyone knows how to put a pup tent together."

"We don't have pup tents in the Financial District."

"And yet the bottom line remains the same. Electronics are not allowed."

"I wasn't—"

"A simple rule. The children understand this rule."

"But—"

Lucy cleared her throat. "We're communing with nature, Jack. Enjoying everything God gave us. Didn't you enjoy the trail ride here? The scenery is pretty stupendous. What about that campfire stew and those sweet potato biscuits? Our cook used to be a chef at a Michelin three-star restaurant. He's a volunteer, too."

"The meal was delicious." He nodded. "To tell you the truth, I might have enjoyed the ride, if it were two hours shorter."

"Nonetheless, you were warned. No electronics."

"Technically, I wasn't using my phone. It was a tutorial on putting up tents that I downloaded earlier." He glanced at the pile of tarp and poles in front of him once more and grimaced.

"I know an electronics infraction when I see one, Mr. Harris."

"Are we back to, Mr. Harris?" He turned and met her gaze. "How's the head?"

Lucy gingerly touched her fingers to the back of her head. "I'm perfectly fine. It doesn't even hurt."

"Then why are your eyes crossed?"

She stiffened. "They are not." Refusing to be distracted, she held out her palm. "If you're trying to earn brownie points with the electronics police, it's not working."

"Apparently you're feeling better." He stared at her outstretched hand and held up two fingers. "How many fingers?"

"Two." Lucy stretched her hand even closer to him.

He stepped back. "What if my aunt tries to reach me?"

"The sympathy card won't work, either. Meredith has all the ranch numbers. They'll contact us immediately. We even have a two-way radio for emergencies." She put her hands on her hips. "We've been doing this for a long time, Mr. Harris. We have a contingency plan for everything."

"No electronics," he repeated. "Do you mind telling me how you're going to wake everyone up in the morning? And what about breakfast?"

"Actually, I will have the pleasure of rousing our camp. I wake daily at dawn automatically. It's a little-known talent of mine."

"Why am I not surprised?" he muttered.

"Pardon me?"

Jack knelt down to smooth the ground cloth. "And meals?"

"We have a fire permit for the evening campfires, and our cook will be using a camp stove with a propane tank. Authentic meals, I'm afraid. Right down to the coffee."

Jack took a deep breath.

"Now, may I have your phone?" She paused. "And your watch."

He stood and hesitantly placed the cell in her hand. When their hands touched, Lucy stepped back and looked away. How could a simple touch be so potent? This was new territory for her and she was admittedly confused.

"What happens at night?" Jack finally asked.

"At night?"

"While we're sleeping. If there's an emergency. Coyotes, wolves, bears." He frowned and glanced around at the looming dark shadows of the woods that surrounded them, as though evaluating the merit of her words. "Or illness."

"We have security. I hired two wranglers to watch the camp during the night to ensure our site is secure, and because I am aware that kids will be kids. I don't want any problems while I sleep. They'll ride to the ranch in the morning and be back again at night."

"That was a three-hour ride to get here."

"They took the shortcut on the other side of the woods. It connects with the main road."

"Any special reason we had to commune with nature this far out, as opposed to, say, one hour on the trail?" Jack glanced at her. "I would have been okay with the one-hour back route. I've got aches where I didn't even know I could have aches."

"I thought your aunt said you were experienced in the saddle."

"I was. A long time ago."

"Where did you ride?"

"Aunt Meredith's stable used to be filled with horses. My brother and I spent every summer in the saddle."

"Good memories?"

"Yeah, the best. I would have savored them more if I'd only known."

"Known what?" Lucy asked.

He shook his head, dismissing the subject.

"Well, if it's any consolation, there are actually

other reasons for being this far out. I'll explain when it starts raining."

She followed his gaze when he glanced up at the night sky. A stretch of deep blue-black edged with the fading orange of the setting sun filled the skies. Around them, the only sounds were the katydids singing and the muffled chatter of tent conversations.

"Doesn't look like rain to me," he finally said.

"All meteorological indicators point to rain tomorrow afternoon, and it's going to be a gully washer."

"A what?"

"I'll explain that tomorrow, as well," she said. "In the meantime, relax. Enjoy yourself, and I'll have Rue drop off some ibuprofen."

He stared at the pile of poles and fabric at his feet. "Enjoy. Yeah, I'll get right on that."

"Would you like some help with your tent?" Lucy asked.

"It's a simple pup tent. I ought to be able to put it together myself." He turned his head to look at the other tents, all efficiently raised and ready for the night.

"I'll send Dub out to help you. Please escort him back to the camp wagon when he's done."

"You're telling me that a first-grader knows how to put up a tent?"

"Kindergartener." She nodded. "And yes, Dub is extremely intuitive."

"Great. First undermined by a chicken, now I'll be schooled by a five-year-old."

"We're all about sharing our special skills here."

"Are you?"

"Yes. Oh, and do hurry, or you're going to miss dessert. Dub is so excited about ice cream and cake that he's sitting in that wagon talking to the cook nonstop."

"Ice cream?"

"Anything is possible at Big Heart Ranch."

"It's got to cost a fortune to bring ice cream out here in the middle of nowhere in July. That's how you allocate donations?"

"Put away your calculator heart, Mr. Harris." She pointed a finger at him. "This did not come out of our budget. The mayor of Timber donated the ice cream. They're bringing it out on dry ice with the Ute, from the main road."

"The mayor?"

"Yes. He supports our ranch one hundred percent. It helps that he owns an ice cream parlor, as well."

"We better get the Dubster over here to save me, so he can have his cake and ice cream."

"Will do." She turned to leave, but then stopped and faced him. "I didn't thank you for coming to my assistance this afternoon. Thank you."

Jack nodded without meeting her gaze. Head down, he shifted position as though unaccustomed to thanks, and tucked his hands into his front pockets. This was a vulnerable side of the man she hadn't seen. It was oddly attractive.

"And thank you for praying with Dub earlier. I have no idea if you're a praying man, but Dub needed that. A male role model and all."

"Me? A role model?" He scoffed. "I don't think so."

"You underestimate yourself, and you were great with Dub."

"Hmm. Was I? Aunt Meri had me in church all the time when I was Dub's age."

"And now?"

"I seem to have misplaced a good excuse for why I haven't given God the time of day."

She nodded slowly. "You're very close to your aunt, aren't you?"

"I owe her a lot. My aunt gave me hope when I needed it most."

"She gave us hope, too. Once she got on board, the entire community followed. Now that's exactly what we offer in return at the ranch. Hope. No one understands that more than Meredith Brisbane."

"My aunt is getting older. I'm not sure about her decision-making ability anymore."

"It isn't necessary for you to keep reminding me that this isn't personal. I get that, Jack. All I'm saying is that you shouldn't rule out the possibility that God has a hand in all our lives—yours, mine, your aunt's and Dub's. Have you considered that you might be here for a reason, and perhaps it has nothing to do with Big Heart Ranch's donation?"

"You really believe that?"

"You've been with us only twenty-four hours, and already I'm sensing a change in you."

His gaze met hers, and for once the gray eyes were without shutters. He stared for a long moment as if searching for something. Maybe the same thing she was—trying to figure out what was happening between them.

"I believe anything is possible, Jack," she whispered. "And trust me, that thought scares me as much as it does you."

# Chapter Five

"Rise and shine."

Jack groaned and opened his eyes. This was probably the strangest dream he'd ever had—bordering on a nightmare when he realized that it was Lucy Maxwell's voice. He smelled bacon, too. *Odd.* Patting the ground beside him, he searched for his phone, but his fingers only came up with the cool, damp fabric of the ground cloth.

He blinked and realized where he was. In a tent. On the Big Heart Ranch epic trail ride and campout. In the middle of nowhere, Oklahoma. Without his cell phone or his watch.

"Mr. Jack?" A soft pummeling on his tent wall ensued. "Time to rise and shine. Miss Lucy said so a long time ago. Didn't you hear her?"

Dub Lewis.

"I'm up."

"Hurry. You missed breakfast and we gotta start the scavenger hunt."

"I missed breakfast?" Jack rubbed his eyes. But he was sure it was only minutes ago that he'd heard Lucy's voice.

"Are you coming?"

"I am. Be right there, Dub. Don't move."

"Yes, sir. But I have to make a trip down to the outhouse. And I gots to go bad."

"Go. I'll be right there."

"I'm not allowed to go by myself. I have to go with my buddy." There was a long pause. "That's you."

"Okay. Hang on a minute." Jack unzipped his sleeping bag, tried to stand and fell over in a tangle. "Oomph."

"You okay, Mr. Jack?"

"I'm fine," he muttered. Once again he automatically reached for his phone to check both the time and the temperature. No phone. *Right*. Drill Sergeant Maxwell had confiscated it.

He grabbed his paddock boots, unzipped the tent and crawled out, managing to hit his head on a tent pole. "Ouch."

"Mr. Jack, your tent is lopsided."

"Yeah. I got up in the night and forgot I was in a tent and bent the pole. Maybe we can fix that today."

"Okay."

"How did you sleep, Dub?"

"Good, until the big boys came in."

"Big boys?"

"Yeah. Stewie and Henry. They're twelve. They're my brothers here at the ranch. We live in the same house. Miss Lucy made them sleep in the wagon 'cause they were naughty."

"Oh, yeah?"

Dub nodded. "They tried to scare me with creepy stories, but I plugged my ears."

"Good for you."

Jack glanced down at the little man outside his tent. Today he wore jeans, a striped T-shirt and the red sneakers he favored. A small backpack was slung over his shoulder. The boy wriggled in an antsy dance, moving back and forth from one foot to another.

"I guess you're ready to go."

"Uh-huh." Dub shot ahead down the path to the creek.

"Wait for me. Those woods can be dangerous," Jack called. "Stop moving. Stand right there."

"You missed the meeting," Dub announced when Jack caught up. "Miss Lucy said she tried to wake you up, but you yelled at her."

"I did?"

"Yeth. She said sometimes it's better to let people sleep."

"I had a hard time falling asleep," he muttered. If he'd had his phone, his alarm would have ensured an early rising and that he didn't miss anything. Plus, he'd know the forecast. The weather app on his phone would have provided the humidity, UV index, wind factor and temperature. Without an information overload, the world seemed off.

His gaze scanned the sky, which held low layered clouds. Okay, fine. No weather app needed today. Nothing said rain louder than cumulonimbus or nimbostratus clouds. Yesterday he would have said that it was impossible for the humidity to get any higher. Yet today it was so thick, he could easily swim down to the creek. Muggy Oklahoma air had drowned out the scent of pine and campfire cooking.

Yes. It was going to rain. All part of Lucy's nefarious plot to annoy him.

"Ouch." Dub slapped a hand to his forearm.

"You okay?"

"Yeth. Just a skeeter."

"Skeeter?" Jack frowned. "Oh, a mosquito. Don't scratch the bite."

Dub nodded. "Miss Lucy passed out the scavenger hunt papers. I gots one for us. She said that if it rains, we're going through the woods to the other side."

"What's on the other side?"

Dub shrugged.

"Anything else?" Jack asked.

"Watch out for poison ivy. Some of the boys already have the itches. Miss Lucy says she's real allergic to poison ivy. So we should go see the general if we get allergic, not her."

Jack picked up a long stick near the edge of the woods and tapped it on the ground, testing its sturdiness. Then he began to strip the bark.

"What's that for?" Dub asked.

"To keep us out of the poison ivy."

"What's poison ivy look like?"

"It looks like a plant."

"But Mr. Jack, the woods have lots of plants."

"You're right, Dub. Which is why we have to be extra careful. It's a tricky plant."

"How will we know?"

"Poison ivy has three leaves." Jack stopped and glanced around as they walked deeper into the dense brush. "Wow, there's a lot of poison ivy in these woods." He crouched down to inspect the brush. "See?" Jack nodded toward the foliage and used the stick to point out the three-leaf configuration. "This is what I'm talking about."

When Dub reached out a hand toward the plant, Jack's arm shot out to hold him back. "You can't touch. At all. It has oil that gets on your clothes and your skin and causes all sorts of itchy problems." Jack stood. "We'll stay on the trail. But don't touch anything that looks like this."

"Three. Three. Three," Dub repeated as he headed down the trail. Then he stopped and glanced around. "You hear that noise?"

"July in Oklahoma means singing bugs." Jack reluctantly grinned. One more thing he'd nearly forgotten. "Those are the cicadas. They sing in the daytime, and the katydids sing at night."

Dub's amused laughter rang out. "Singing bugs."

At the end of the trail, the underbrush thinned and finally separated to reveal two outhouses on the right and a bubbly tree-lined creek straight ahead.

Jack entered one outhouse door and Dub the

other. When they emerged, Jack pointed to the water. "Let's wash in the creek."

Dub dipped his hands in the water and swished them around. Then he stood and stepped back, eyes wide. "I saw something move in there." Excitement laced his voice, and he splashed his hands in the water again. "Maybe it was a fish."

Jack stepped closer and knelt on the muddy shale stones of the creek bank. "Pollywogs."

"What's a pollywog?"

"Those are baby frogs. Little swimmers."

Again, Dub laughed at this new word. Fascinated, he knelt at the creek's edge, scooting close to Jack, eyes on the water for long minutes. When he started to slip forward, Jack grabbed a handful of T-shirt and pulled him back.

Dub turned, eyes wide. "I almost fell in."

"I know. You have to be careful." Jack stood. "Ready to go?"

"Uh-huh. But don't you want your breakfast?"

"What?"

Dub pulled off his backpack and brought out a plastic bag with toast and bacon and offered it to Jack.

"Where'd this come from?"

"I asked the cook to save some for you, and he did."

"Dub, thank you." Jack stared at the little guy in wonder, touched by the gesture. "Come on. Let's find a chair."

"A chair?"

"Yeah. See those tree stumps. We can sit there."

"Poison ivy?"

"It's safe." Jack sat and pulled the bacon from the bag. "Want some?"

"Yeth, please."

Jack handed the bag to Dub.

"It sure is pretty out here, isn't it Mr. Jack?" Dub chewed slowly, savoring the bacon. His little feet tapped on the long grass that grew around the stump as he glanced around.

"Yeah, Dub, it is." Jack's gaze followed Dub's. Mature trees lined the creek, shading the frothy water from the sun's rays. The creek wound through the fingers of a willow whose roots were embedded in the bank and covered in moss before the stream moved over fallen logs at a leisurely pace. As the water passed over rock and shale, a tinkling song reached out to those who listened.

The song of the creek settled between Jack and Dub as they ate.

"Do you like kids, Mr. Jack?"

"Huh?" Jack turned to Dub. "Where did that come from?"

"I was just wondering. Stewie said you look sorta like you don't like kids."

"What?"

"'Cause you don't smile."

"I don't smile?" Jack pondered the words. "I guess I think a lot."

"What do you think about?"

"Everything. Too much of everything."

"Do you have a mom and dad?"

Jack nodded.

"Sisters and brothers?"

"I used to have a brother. He was a lot like you. Smart and happy and he talked all the time. I liked to listen to him talk." Jack swallowed back emotion that threatened. Emotion he thought he'd buried long ago.

"What happened to him?" Dub asked.

"He died."

Dub was silent for minutes, then he slid off the stump and walked over and placed a hand on Jack's arm. "Don't be sad," he said solemnly. "I'm your buddy. You have me."

"I, ah… Thanks, Dub."

"Maybe you can meet my sisters."

"Maybe."

"I'll ask Miss Lucy. Maybe you can take us for ice cream, too."

"Maybe." Jack smiled.

"When can I ride Grace?"

"Kid, you segue faster than a trader on Wall Street."

"Huh?"

"Never mind. Do you have boots?"

"Boots? No. I have sneakers. Miss Lucy calls them tennis shoes, but I don't know how to play tennis."

"We need to get you a pair of boots like mine before you can ride Grace." Jack glanced at Dub's sneakers. "Can I see one?"

Dub frowned. "You want to see my shoe?"

"Yeah."

Dub slipped off a sneaker and offered it to Jack.

"Size twelve." He handed the shoe back. "Now, where's that scavenger hunt list?"

Dub fished a damp and crumpled paper from his pocket and handed it over. Jack chuckled and smoothed the sheet on his leg.

"Okay, here's what we have to find. A heart-shaped stone. A snakeskin. A feather. Tree bark. A pine cone. A green leaf and a dry brown leaf. Seeds. A stick shaped like a letter. Oh, and something red."

The sound of campers marching through the woods interrupted their conversation. Jack recognized one of the voices. *Lucy.* He feigned deep concentration with the list.

"Mr. Harris, how lovely of you to get up at the crack of noon," she called out.

"I don't have a watch, so I don't know what time it is," he returned without looking up.

"I did try to wake you, but you threw a shoe in my general direction."

"Yeah, sorry about that. Nothing personal. I'm not responsible for my actions when I'm asleep."

"I'll make note of that sad story. In the meantime, Dub can probably teach you how to tell time by looking at the sun. Right, Dub?"

"Yeth, Miss Lucy."

Jack grudgingly met her gaze as she breezed past with two boys at her heels.

"You'll have to get moving if you want to win." She smiled indulgently at him. "Early bird catches the worm," she taunted.

"Nope. There isn't a single worm on the list," he muttered.

"That's Stewie and Henry," Dub said.

"Those boys with her? Miss Lucy has two buddies?"

"Uh-huh."

"Figures. Overachiever."

"What's that mean?"

"It means that we better get going." Jack shoved the rest of the toast in his mouth and held up the empty plastic bag. "Here. You hold this for our scavenger hunt stuff."

"Okay."

"We're going to find everything on that list, Dub."

"We have to do it faster than Miss Lucy."

"Yeah. We will. Don't worry. I have a long history of winning."

"I dunno. She's good."

"Miss Lucy might be good, but Mr. Jack is better." He offered Dub a fist bump, and the little guy grinned as he touched his small fist to Jack's big one.

Jack pointed to an area to the right. "Look. A red leaf."

"I see it. I see it." Dub grabbed the leaf and put it in the bag, grinning.

"Now what?"

"We're going to unexplored territory. Where Miss Lucy hasn't been."

"Huh?"

"We're crossing that creek, Dub."

Dub blinked. "It's cold and deep, and very, very scary."

"You're going to ride on my back."

"But you'll get cold."

"It's already at least eighty-five degrees. I don't mind a little cold water."

"What if we fall?" Dub looked at him, his lower lip trembling. "I don't how to swim."

Jack crouched down and met the boy's wide blue eyes. "Do you trust me?"

Dub sucked in his lips and nodded.

"Okay, then climb on my back." Jack grunted as Dub hopped on and clung tightly. "Hold on tight, buddy."

When Jack splashed through the shallow creek to the other side, Dub started to giggle. Jack splashed harder, stomping through the water, inciting more laughter. His heart swelled with something he hadn't felt in years. Pure joy.

"There you go." He eased the boy down to the ground. "Now you find a piece of tree bark and I'll find that heart-shaped stone."

"Yes, sir, Mr. Jack."

Jack chuckled, then suddenly paused as reality set in. His little buddy was beginning to grow on him.

That couldn't be a good thing. Could it?

Lucy stood very still watching Jack Harris.

He was stretched on the ground beneath the shade of a redbud tree with a ball cap over his eyes. His head rested on a rolled-up sleeping bag, and his arms were crossed over his broad chest.

Ugh. Why did the man look so good? They'd been out here for two days now, and lack of hygiene was already evident on everyone except him. There was no doubt that she looked appalling, and smelled like eau de insect repellent and Oklahoma dirt, as well.

Lucy pushed her Stetson from her head until it hung by the leather cord down her back. She finger combed her hair, tucking it behind her ears, pretending that the preening would make a difference.

"Jack?"

He slowly raised the visor of the cap from his face and eyed her with suspicion. "Yes, Drill Sergeant?"

"Why aren't you napping in your tent?"

"My tent doesn't like me." He dropped the cap over his face.

"I see." She crossed her arms and bit her lip, hoping for a natural opening to the next topic on her mind.

"Was there something else?" he mumbled.

"Um, yes, actually. I want to talk to you about Dub."

"Am I in trouble again?"

"You tell me."

Jack offered a dramatic sigh and sat up.

"Dub says you agreed to go for ice cream with him and his sisters, and that you're going to let him ride Grace."

"I believe the operative word I used was *maybe*."

"There's something you need to understand. While children pretend to understand maybe, the reality is that there is no 'maybe' in a child's vocabulary," Lucy said. "There is only 'you promised' and 'you lied.'"

Jack blinked and frowned. "Oh."

"Yes. Oh. So I trust you will follow through and keep your promises."

"I can do that." He nodded. "By the way, don't forget to pencil me in."

Panic tap-danced in her stomach at his words. "Pencil you in for what?" She stared blankly at him.

"Remember what Rue said? Walk a mile in

your shoes. I'd like to spend the day with you in your office."

"I can provide you with any number of ranch financials or paperwork you want to review. Transparent is my middle name."

"No. I want to spend the day understanding what the director does."

Lucy took a calming breath, imagining Jack in her itty-bitty messy office. She wouldn't be able to breathe with him that close. "Is that necessary?"

"I think so."

"Fine," Lucy muttered. Which meant that she'd find a way to prevent that from ever happening in her lifetime. She turned on her heel. "But for now, you might want to head over to the field. We're dividing up into teams for softball."

"Seriously? We've been going nonstop since what I believe was 6:00 a.m. I don't have a watch, so I'm not sure." He paused. "First there was the scavenger hunt, followed immediately by the hike from—"

Lucy cleared her throat loudly and swung back to face him. "Language, Mr. Harris."

"What? The hike from my nightmares."

"You're a big-shot attorney. I bet you usually work from dawn to dusk. So what's with the whining about long hours?"

"Yeah, I do—at a desk, with an ergonomic chair, and climate-controlled air."

"What kind of attorney are you anyhow?"

"An extremely boring one. Contract law."

"Quite lucrative, I imagine."

"Imagine away," he said as he adjusted his ball cap. "Just remember that I'm not Mr. Lucrative anymore."

Her eyes rounded, and she gestured wildly with her hands. "You didn't think I was assessing your financial worth, did you?"

"It wouldn't be the first time."

Lucy choked. "Oh, my, my, my. That ego of yours is so enormous, it's a wonder you can stand upright."

"Okay, sorry. I might have jumped to conclusions based on past experiences."

"You think?" She shook her head. "All I was getting at was that you invested years and money in your career and climbed the corporate ladder only to give it away?"

"I still own a walkup in the city and have a gym membership that doesn't expire for twenty-four months."

She laughed. "That's a long way to go for aerobics."

"True. When clearly I can get the same thing here for free, right?"

"Right. So what's the plan?"

"I don't follow."

"Eventually you're going realize that Big Heart Ranch is not a shady fly-by-night outfit. So what's the plan after that?"

"There is no plan. I'm here to help my aunt," he said.

"No plan?"

"It doesn't take a genius to figure out that you're big into plans, Madame Director, but I'm trying to leave my options open. Go with the flow."

"When will you go with the flow back to New York?"

"In a rush to get rid of me?"

"You city folk all get tired of playing cowboy and eventually head back to wherever you came from. I've seen it enough times."

"No bitterness there," Jack muttered.

Lucy stared at him. "What did you say?"

"Sounds like you've had some history with temporary cowboys."

"We're talking about you. Not me."

Jack stood and dusted off his pants. "My ticket is open-ended."

Lucy ignored the comment. "So, you and Dub have really bonded, haven't you?"

He turned around and stared at her. "Have we?"

"It certainly seems that way."

"You gave me an assignment, and I take my assignments very seriously."

"An assignment."

"Was that the wrong answer? Lucy, Dub is my buddy. What else do you want?"

"I want you to be very careful." Lucy said the

words softly as Dub approached them with a grin on his face and a blue ribbon pinned to his chest.

She addressed the little boy. "Congratulations again, Dub. You did a great job with the scavenger hunt."

"Not just me. Mr. Jack, too. We hunted on the other side of the creek. It's a secret." He began to giggle, hands over his mouth.

Lucy glanced from Dub to Jack. Though Jack's face remained impassive, his eyes sparkled with amusement at Dub's words. The man could run, but he couldn't hide from what was happening to him.

"Can I have the treasures we collected, Miss Lucy?"

"Absolutely, but keep that snakeskin in the plastic bag, okay?" Again she looked between them. "You two were the only ones who found the snakeskin."

"We're real good. Right, Dub?" Jack said.

Dub nodded and approached Jack. "Here, Mr. Jack, this is for you." Dub opened his hand, where the heart-shaped stone rested in his small palm.

With a broad smile, Jack took the stone from Dub's little hand. "Thanks, buddy."

Lucy's heart melted. Oh, this wasn't good. Not at all. What was she thinking? Dub was falling for Jack Harris. Soon he'd be tired of Oklahoma and back to his life in New York. And little Dub would be left with a broken heart.

Jack stared at the stone, a tender expression on his face. He slowly lifted his eyes, and his gaze met hers. When Lucy's stomach did a little flip-flop, she knew she was in trouble. Dub wasn't the only one who might be falling for the temporary cowboy.

# Chapter Six

"Come on, Maxwell. Bases are loaded. This is your chance," Jack said from behind home plate. "Look sharp."

"Jack, don't coach her. She's on the opposite team!" Rue Butterfield called out from the pitcher's mound.

"Coach! In his dreams. The man is trying to rattle me," Lucy said as she warmed up, swinging the bat in an arc with a fierce deliberation. She turned and glared at him before lowering the brim of her red-team ball cap and getting back into position.

Jack grinned and flipped his own blue-team cap around until the bill was to the back, before he squatted down and punched the center of his catcher's mitt for good measure. For a micromanaging director, Lucy sure was cute. Distractingly so, in her jeans and red boots. Who played softball in cowboy boots? He chuckled and forced himself to focus on the pitcher. All Rue had to do was strike Lucy out, and the red team would be shut out.

On the mound, General Rue Butterfield began to wind up. Clearly, the general knew her way around a pitching mound. She stood with her left leg slightly elevated, followed by the synchronous movement of her hip as she released the ball.

It flew through the air toward Lucy, faster than a homing missile.

*Crack!*

Whoa! The woman could bat!

Jack jumped up to keep his eye on the ball as it sailed impossibly high and far. He blinked. It seemed apparent he'd underestimated this particular batter.

"Long fly ball," someone called out. Lucy dropped the bat and headed to first, red boots moving faster than he imagined the cowgirl could run.

"Way to make something happen," one of the teenagers on the red team yelled. The chants of support became louder as each runner rounded bases and headed home.

"Take 'er home, Lucy! Take 'er home!" another player called.

"Go! Go! Go!" Dub screamed from his spot on the sidelines. His normally pale complexion was ruddy with the exertion.

Rue backed up and positioned herself to catch the ball the outfielder tossed to her, just as Lucy passed third, her eye intent on home.

Jack cupped his hands around his mouth. "Slide! Slide! You can do it, Lucy!"

Lucy dove at the same time Jack caught the ball Rue threw to him. Red dust filled the air in a cloud, making it impossible to determine the outcome.

"Safe!" the umpire called, arms crossing and then spreading wide.

Lucy stood, a goofy grin on her face, along with a film of dusty red clay. She smiled at him and rubbed her chin with a hand, revealing a bright red abrasion where her face had kissed the ground.

"Nice job, Jeter," Jack said. "Uh, you cut your lip and your chin is bleeding, as well."

"All part of the job," she said. "All part of the job."

"No, really. It's bleeding," he said.

"I'm fine." She lifted her fingers to her face, carefully touching the area, and grimaced.

"Right. I've heard that song somewhere before," he muttered.

"Jack, you seem to be under the impression you are on Lucy's team," Rue observed as she approached from the field, her mitt tucked beneath her arm. She pulled a well-worn copy of the rule book from her back pocket. "Do you need to read this?"

Jack laughed. "Not necessary, General. I have a firm policy of always rooting for the underdog. Another facet of my diverse moral compass."

"Moral compass? You should have been a politician," Lucy panted as she worked hard to catch her breath. She stood staring at him with indignation flushing her face. "And I am not an underdog. You started rooting for me so you'd be on the winning side in your mind."

Jack chuckled, unwilling to admit that rooting for Lucy sort of came out of nowhere. He couldn't help himself.

Rue glanced at Lucy. "Nicely done, dear, but you need medical attention."

Overhead light streaked across the darkening summer sky, followed by the ferocious roar of thunder.

"It will have to wait," Lucy said, her gaze fixed on the fast-moving black clouds above as thunder ripped the air again moments later.

Dub rocketed into the air from his position on the batter's bench and screamed, "Thunder!" His voice quivered.

"Easy, Dub. Easy," Lucy soothed. She shook her head. "Those clouds are moving quickly, but the flash-to-bang count says the heart of that storm is still two miles away. We should have enough time to get to safety. Barely."

Jack met Lucy's gaze. "Did you minor in meteorology in college?" he asked.

"You've got to stay keenly tuned in to the weather when camping. Especially in Oklahoma. This storm was only supposed to be precipitation. Once again I was trumped by Mother Nature." She put her hands around her mouth. "Game called due to weather! Pack up your gear and grab your horses. We are out of here in five."

Groans went up as players left the field and jogged toward the tents.

"What do you mean the game is called? We were about to win," Jack said.

"When pigs fly. My team was about to win," she smoothly replied before turning to Dub. "Get in the wagon quickly, and put on your rain slicker and seat belt."

"Yeth, Miss Lucy."

Then she pointed to Jack. "You'll need to roll up your tent and pack. You have five or six minutes."

"Five minutes? You've got to be kidding. It took me four hours to put the thing up."

A glance at the sky confirmed her words. Large drops began to sail through the air and splatter on them. "Jack, I'm serious here. We leave as a group in five. Any longer and we'll increase the risk of being struck by lightning. Get Grace packed up, but don't ride her."

"Why not?"

"Visibility is going to be an issue, and we don't want any injuries. To horses or humans. Simply keep her calm."

"Where exactly is safety?" he asked.

"There's another route that will take us around the creek. We can make it in ten minutes."

"Make it where?" He turned around. "Lucy?"

The director had disappeared. Five minutes later, when she blew on the giant silver whistle that hung around her neck, he was still struggling with his tent poles.

"Line up!" she called.

"Jack, do you need help?" Rue asked as she straightened her clear plastic rain slicker and pulled the hood up over her silver curls.

He held up the plastic tent poles. "Why is it these things never go back in the package the way you found them?"

Rue only laughed. In under a minute she had the tent and poles neatly tucked into the pouch. "Practice, dear. Practice."

"Uh, thanks. Why aren't we waiting out the storm?" he asked the physician.

She shook her head. "We won't last the storm, not to mention that we're a target for a lightning strike out here in the open. Put on your slicker and prepare for the worst. This is a real Oklahoma gully washer."

"Gully washer again," he muttered.

"Indeed. The water moves fast and creates a dangerous torrent as it travels across the hard clay. Through the woods is the backup plan."

"To grandmother's house we go?"

"Something like that," Rue said as she flicked on her flashlight. "Follow me."

Lucy blew the whistle yet again, and all heads turned toward the director. "We will be walking our horses very carefully. Stay calm and they will, too." She pulled the hood on her cherry-red rain slicker over her hair as rainfall steadily increased, along with the wind.

"Once we get through the woods and arrive at the barn, stable your horse and wipe them down!" Now Lucy was yelling to be heard over the storm. "After you lock the stall, meet General Butterfield at the front of the barn for head count."

The clopping of horses' hooves and the steady drumming of falling rain provided the backdrop for the campers walking through the dark woodland trail. Grace shook her head, tossing moisture from her mane as the rain sluiced down her broad face each time there was a gap in the tree coverage overhead.

Jack shivered and pulled up his shirt collar against the water that ran down his back. The sweatshirt he'd shrugged over his head back at camp was already heavy with moisture. "How far is this place?" he asked Rue.

"A straight shot. Ten minutes at most." She looked him up and down, a frown on her face. "Where's your rain slicker?"

"I might have forgotten to bring one."

Rue chuckled. "And your flashlight?"

"Confiscated. It was on my phone."

"Ah, right, city boy." She thrust an old-fashioned battery-operated flashlight into his hands. "Here. I have a spare. Not as cool as yours, I'm sure, but it works."

"Thanks, Rue." He shined the light toward the

back of the procession. "Where's Dub and the chuck wagon?"

"The chuck wagon detoured straight to the main road and around. They'll meet us there." She smiled and patted his arm. "Don't worry about your buddy. He's safe."

Jack paused at Rue's words. Yeah, he was worried. Only a week, and already he was attached to the little guy. Attached and also responsible for him, even though he'd promised himself never again. There went his good intentions.

"I'm going to the rear to round up the stragglers," Rue said. She clucked her tongue and led her horse away from him.

A sudden gust of wind and rain nearly pulled Jack's ball cap off, before he repositioned it snugly on his head and wiped moisture from his face with the back of his hand.

"How do you like the weather?"

Jack jumped at the words and turned to see Lucy. "You're kind of like a ninja, aren't you? You appear silently out of the darkness." He glanced at her dark chestnut horse. "Even your horse is stealthy."

"Right. Cowgirl ninja and her faithful horse, Blaze."

Yet again, a streak of lightning lit up the sky overhead, followed by thunder. Grace whinnied nervously, and her hooves clopped on the wet ground in a fretful two-step next to him. Jack grabbed the reins tighter and ran a hand over the horse's forehead. "Easy, girl," he crooned.

"Grace doing okay?" Lucy asked.

"Actually, Grace seems to really like the rain. It's that noise she's not crazy about."

When Grace nodded and nickered in agreement, both Lucy and Jack laughed.

"How safe are we from lightning in the woods?" he asked Lucy.

"Safer than we were in that open field. Safer than if there were only one or two trees. I've been praying since that first lightning strike, Jack. That's all I know to do when the going gets tough. That and move quickly."

The trail narrowed and Jack pushed back the wet, low-hanging leaves of a maple and held them for Lucy and several campers to pass through. Then he blinked at the sight before him.

Not far ahead was a huge two-story log home lit up like a candle in the storm to welcome them. A rust-colored barn was angled to the left of the house. The chuck wagon had been parked in the drive, right in front of the house.

"What is this? You've been holding out on me," Jack said when he caught up to Lucy. "This was here all along?"

She stopped and they stood side by side, staring at the shelter from the storm straight ahead. "Don't get too excited. It's an empty house."

"An empty house in the middle of nowhere?"

"That's right."

"Running water?" he asked.

"Yes. Well water."

"Electricity?"

"Yes."

"What do you use this for?"

"I don't use the place, although it's kept stocked with emergency supplies. Canned food, candles, powdered milk, blankets and first-aid supplies. The usual doomsday stuff."

"Just in case of a zombie apocalypse?"

"Exactly," Lucy said. She turned to him with a slight smile.

He stared, fascinated, as the rain landed on her long eyelashes. When moisture ran down her nose, Jack was unable to resist reaching out a finger to catch the errant drops.

Lucy's dark eyes rounded at his touch, yet she didn't move away.

"Sorry. You were dripping."

For the longest moment, they stared at each other as they stood beneath the branches of the tree, the rain falling around them like a curtain. Jack leaned forward slightly.

"We don't want to go there, Jack," Lucy murmured, her voice a shaky whisper.

He stepped back.

She was right. Again.

Jack gripped the reins in his hand and turned toward the house, thankful for the shadows and questioning his impulsive gesture. Questioning his sanity when Lucy Maxwell was around.

They walked in silence across the clearing, getting closer and closer to the two-story structure.

"Where did it come from?" he finally asked.

"Wh-what?"

"The house."

"It's mine."

"You built a house that you never use?"

"I already said that."

Did he detect annoyance in her voice?

"I don't get it. What am I missing here?" Jack asked as they edged nearer to the property.

"What's to get?" She shrugged. "Sometimes the boot drops, plans change and you move on."

Something like nostalgia—or was it regret?—crossed Lucy's face as she stared at the house.

Jack nodded, his gaze assessing the ranch director. This was all very odd. He'd get to the bottom of this house-in-the-woods mystery eventually.

"We'll divide up into groups, and you'll be sleeping on the floor in your sleeping bag," Lucy continued.

"My own room?"

"Nice try."

"And yet, there are no tent poles to deal with. No mosquitos biting or katydids to sing all night." He stopped at a sudden thought. "I don't suppose there's cable and internet."

"The ban on electronics is still in place. Our

roughing it simply got a little less rough." She looked at him, her eyes sparkling. "Wait until you see the fireplace in the great room. We can take turns roasting marshmallows tonight."

"S'mores?"

"I never got to be a Girl Scout, but I do understand the importance of s'mores. The cook will have plenty of supplies." She squirmed and scratched her arm.

"Poison ivy?"

"A touch."

"I can go get the general. She's not far behind."

"No. I'm fine. No big deal." She nodded toward the barn. "Come on. First things first. Head count, and then I need to get the horses settled for the night."

"Is there feed in that barn?"

"Of course. Everything is ready for the animals. All part of Plan B."

"How did you know we'd need one?" Jack asked.

"My life is an extended series of Plan B's. I've learned to stay one step ahead of them."

He frowned. "That's too bad."

"Is it?"

"You just said you live with a permanent worst-case-scenario agenda."

She frowned for a moment and pursed her lips. "I like to think of myself as extremely well-prepared."

"No. You're a pessimist who plans for failure."

"That's neither true nor fair. You hardly know me. At least not well enough to judge me." Lucy released a sigh. "I happen to be a very positive and optimistic person, unlike you, interviewing campers in your spare time, hoping to uncover some evil plot at Big Heart Ranch."

"I'm being friendly."

"Perhaps we can agree to disagree on this matter."

"Sure. But I'm still right," Jack murmured.

For long moments the only sound was Blaze's soft snort and Grace's whinny as rain continued to fall in silent sheets.

They crossed the gravel yard in front of the house and stopped outside the barn, where several riders and horses were already waiting. Lucy pulled back the metal slide bar and yanked open the big wooden double doors.

"Is there a light?" Jack asked.

"To your right. On the wall," Lucy said.

He hit the switch, illuminating the huge barn. The place was as nice as the stables at Big Heart Ranch. Hooves clopped on the plank floors as young riders and volunteers led their horses into the dry building. The campers' chatter echoed their relief. Jack also looked forward to getting out of wet clothes.

Lucy led her own horse into a stall at the far end of the barn, grabbed a towel from the stack on a shelf and began to briskly rub down Blaze.

He followed suit and opened the stall next to hers. A towel and brush were ready on a shelf. He removed Grace's tack, and carefully dried it and hung the saddle up to dry out. Grace whinnied and shook her head, sprinkling water everywhere.

"Grace," Jack murmured. "You're giving me a shower." He inspected the horse and brushed down her silky flank.

Minutes later, Rue appeared outside Lucy's stall. "I've done a head count. Everyone is accounted for and in one piece. We have three with poison ivy. I'm glad we're at the lodge tonight."

"The lodge?" Jack asked.

Rue smiled. "A nickname for the house." She turned back to Lucy. "I'll have the affected children shower first, and I'll bag up their clothing."

"Calamine and cortisone cream?" Lucy asked.

"Yes. We have plenty. And good thing—the poison ivy really is out of control this year."

Lucy shook her head, a troubled expression on her face. "I should have had someone up here to spray the grounds before we came."

"Lucy dear, you cannot possibly think of everything. When three children who were previously warned play in the poison ivy, you cannot blame yourself. Mother Nature will win every time."

"Still. I'll have the grounds sprayed before Travis brings his group out next Wednesday."

"Of course you will." Rue smiled and offered an indulgent nod. "We're heading into the lodge then."

"I'll be along shortly," Lucy said.

"Let someone else do the stall check," Rue said as she pulled her hood up over her head again.

"I'll sleep better if I do the job myself."

Rue stared at her and silently shook her head. "Don't take too long. You don't want to miss the treats, or the hot water before it runs out." The general led the line of boys and staff to the front door of the lodge, and they all disappeared inside.

Outside, the rain began to pound on the metal roof of the barn, *rat-a-tat-tat*, like a stranger demanding to be let in.

"Thunder and lightning have stopped," Jack observed. "But the rain is really picking up."

"I suggest you take cover, as well. Head for the house," Lucy said.

"What about you?"

"I'm going to do a visual check of all the horses first, and then I'll be in."

"I'll help you."

"That's not necessary."

"Lucy, how am I going to fill Leo's shoes if you keep turning down my help?"

"Okay, fine." She ran her fingers through the wet tangles of her hair.

Weariness seemed to have settled on her like a heavy blanket, and he found himself longing to ease her burden. Despite their differences, he had to admire the woman. She was always first on the job and last to leave. Her work ethic rivaled any he'd ever seen.

Lucy released a breath and tucked her shoulders back, as if rallying for a second round. "I'm going to inspect the horses. You check the stalls to be sure every horse has sufficient feed and enough water for the night."

"I thought someone did that already."

"We do it again at night check. Those are the rules."

"Seems repetitive, if you ask me."

A smile twitched at her lips. "Ah, yes, but I didn't ask you."

"Touché, Madame Director."

# Chapter Seven

"Ouch," Lucy murmured as Rue dabbed antibiotic ointment on her chin.

"Sorry, dear." Rue stepped back and assessed Lucy's face. "You've had quite a week. A near concussion, cut lip and chin, and now the poison ivy!"

"Yes, but that home run was worth every last scrape and bruise. Did you see Jack's eyes bug out of his head when I knocked that ball to the moon? I'll be savoring that for a long time."

Rue chuckled as she placed the tube of medication on the kitchen counter. She sniffed the air and stepped back. "What is that on your shirt, Lucy?"

Lucy looked down. "Blaze spit up on me."

"I trust you're going to shower tonight?"

"As soon as the hot water tank recovers."

"That may be a while." Rue shook her head. "You look exhausted, dear."

"I'll be fine." As she said the words, her body begged for rest from this very long day. Soon. Very soon.

"Yes. Fine as always," Rue returned with an arched brow. "Now, let's see those rashes."

Lucy slipped off her lightweight, zip-front sweatshirt and stretched out her arms. "So far everything is mild. Thank you for the cortisone cream."

"You're welcome. We're headed back in the morning, right?"

"Late morning. Cook is making Belgian waffles outside with the portable stove before we go."

"Despite the fact that this trip has been a comedy of errors, we certainly have eaten well."

"True that," Lucy said.

The older woman smiled. "You know, if we hadn't had a rainout, I do believe your team might have come close to winning the game."

"Rue. We did win."

"Oh, no, dear, you called the game, and we weren't even close to the fourth inning. We call that a scratch. We'll have to have a rematch."

Lucy groaned. "Scratch? That's not a regulation softball term, Rue."

"Nonetheless—"

Jack popped his head into the kitchen. "Sorry to interrupt this sports discussion, ladies."

"Ah, our catcher. Just in time. You agree with me, right, Jack? That game was a scratch."

"I'll get back to you on that, General." He turned to Lucy. "They've cleaned us out of every last s'more, and it was suggested that I find you to signal the official bedtime roundup."

Lucy pulled her silver whistle from around her neck and held it out to him, her arm limp.

His eyes widened and he stepped back. "The whistle? You want me to take the official whistle?"

"You've certainly earned the privilege, after today," Lucy said.

"I don't know. I'm only a stand-in for Leo," he returned with a wink to Rue, who chuckled.

On impulse, Lucy stepped close and placed the whistle in his hand, then closed his fingers around the shiny metal. "You can do this. I have faith in you, Jack."

Jack's mouth tilted upward. "Thank you, Lucy," he murmured, his other hand closing over hers, his gaze intense, as though they were alone in the room.

Lucy nodded and swallowed, her heart thumping in her chest. She slipped her hand from his and turned to the sink.

"My, my, my," Rue said quietly.

"What?" Lucy overturned a stack of paper cups, righted them and fumbled with the faucet until the water cooperated.

"I had no idea."

"No idea what?" She filled the cup and chugged back the water, nearly choking in the process.

"Nothing, dear. Nothing." Rue gathered the supplies spread over the counter into her medical bag, snapped the brass closure in place and smiled. "Sleep tight."

Even after a shower, sleep remained oddly elusive. Lucy paced back and forth across the wide first-floor porch while the rain continued to patter against the eaves and drip from the gutters, splashing inches away from her feet.

Turning back to one of the two large rockers on the porch, she picked up her blanket and cocooned herself before sinking into the chair's deep seat.

Maybe it was the incident with Jack earlier. But which one? That moment in the woods or the one in the kitchen? What had she been thinking, taking his hand? Lucy Maxwell didn't do impulsive things like that. Hadn't she learned long ago to avoid situations where failure was not an option?

The screen door creaked, and Jack Harris stepped outside while pulling a dark sweatshirt over jeans and a white T-shirt. "May I join you?"

"Jack," she murmured. Just what she didn't need right now.

"Was that a yes?" he asked.

"Sure," she murmured. With the blanket draped around her, Lucy stood and moved to the far end of the porch. "Insomnia?" she asked as she peered into the darkness, working hard to remain nonchalant.

"I suppose so. It's always difficult to sleep when it's raining. Seems like I should be awake and enjoying the sounds."

"That's an interesting way to look at the weather. Where does that come from?"

When he leaned against the rail and rolled up

the sleeves of his sweatshirt, her gaze was irresistibly drawn to him.

"My aunt, I guess. Wow, long time ago." He paused and ran a hand through his disheveled hair, as though struggling to recall distant memories. "I had nightmares often as a kid, and one night they were especially bad. A thunderstorm contributed to the issue, I suppose. Aunt Meri opened the French doors and we sat beneath the eaves, just like this, for hours. Aunt Meri said the storm was a private show from God, just for us." A small smile touched his lips.

"Your aunt is an amazing woman."

Jack nodded and offered a weary smile.

"Why the nightmares?" Lucy asked.

He shrugged and crossed his arms, dismissing the subject. "This is a great house, you know."

Lucy studied his strong profile as he stared out into the night. There were plenty of secrets hidden inside Jack Harris. That was the only thing she knew for certain after a week with the man.

"You're missing a great opportunity here," he mused.

"What opportunity is that?"

Jack turned to face her. "Your lodge is an untapped gold mine that could single-handedly keep your ranch afloat."

"What are you talking about?" Lucy asked, knowing that she probably shouldn't ask questions she didn't want the answer to. An uneasy shiver ran over her when he assessed the house before once again pinning her with his gaze.

"You were going on about cattle and vegetables and a self-sustaining vision for the ranch and all, correct?"

"Your point?"

"A little tweaking and you can rent this place out. Vacation rentals are big right now. Then there's weddings and retreats and small group programs. You know, if you add a few horses you have—"

"A dude ranch!" Lucy said, horror lacing her voice.

"They don't call them dude ranches anymore. Guest ranch is the term. Tourists really love that stuff."

She stiffened with indignation. "I don't think so."

"Why not?"

"Do you know how many guest ranches there are in the state of Oklahoma?"

"Come on, you were the one who said that people pay a small fortune for this kind of outdoor experience."

Lucy sank down into the nearest chair and gripped the wooden arms of the rocker. "I need to keep my big mouth shut."

"Visualize the chuck wagon in front of the house. Add picnic tables, and you've got more authentic Oklahoma experiences for very little overhead." He gestured with a hand, excitement simmering in his voice. "You were right, Lucy. Camping. Trail rides. Outdoor meals. Rustic adventure. They eat it up, and you've got the perfect place sitting empty, waiting for you to tap into."

"They can eat it up somewhere else," she grumbled.

"Are you against making money?"

"No."

"All the profits would go directly back into the organization. Even your accountant would approve."

"Is everything about money with you, Harris?"

"Some people think that's a good thing. And who knows? If this takes off, you don't have to be as dependent on my aunt's donation. On anyone's donation."

"We are not dependent on your aunt's money. We are dependent on God."

He cocked his head. "Then why am I the new Leo?"

"We…we can't finalize our budget until we know what our estimated donations will be."

"With this idea, you never have to worry."

Lucy bit back the response on the end of her tongue and silently counted to five. "We don't worry. Big Heart Ranch belongs to God."

"Great, because I can't see God disapproving of using your resources for the kids. You said you want to be good stewards of the finances."

"But…but…" She struggled with the words, her mouth suddenly dry. "I thought you were here to approve the ranch for the donation."

"I'm here to get an understanding of what you do at the ranch. How the funds are allocated."

"How's that going for you?"

"Lucy, I'm not saying I will or will not approve of the funds. This is apples and oranges. But you should at least think about what I'm saying. My aunt isn't going to be around forever. I'm offering you a way to ensure the ranch will be, and you're telling me that you aren't interested."

"You're twisting my words around. What I said is that I have no interest in any commercial venture that would include this house, Jack."

"What if your sister and Travis are interested?"

Lucy opened her mouth and closed it again. Her stomach dipped, and a queasy, unrestful feeling settled in the pit. It was her house. She longed to stamp her feet. If she had her way, she'd simply knock the place down. Raze it until it was gone, along with any evidence of how naive she'd been. And how her heart and her dreams had been broken into a zillion little pieces. The log house represented a happily-ever-after she'd never have.

"Tell you what," he said. "I'll make this easy. Let me do the legwork. This is the sort of thing I'm good at. I'll present you with my findings and we can go from there."

She frowned, growing more and more annoyed.

"Do we have a deal?"

"Fine. But I do not want a dude ranch here. I can't risk an unsavory presence on the property."

"We can find a way to make this work and keep the two entities separate."

"Can we?" She rubbed absently at the rash on her arms. The skin burned beneath her shirt.

"Sure. Where's your spirit of adventure?" He paused and pinned her with his gaze. "Why weren't you a Girl Scout anyhow?"

Lucy shook her head and looked at him. "You might consider refraining from prying into people's personal lives, Harris."

He offered a distracted nod at her words. "You know, it just occurred to me that maybe your childhood snuffed out any opportunity for being adventurous."

She stiffened. "I'm as adventurous as the next gal."

"So why no Girl Scouts? You sounded sort of bitter when you mentioned it earlier."

"No one shells out money to fosters for frivolous things like Girl Scouts."

"Fosters, huh?" He shook his head. "What happened to your parents, Lucy?" Jack asked quietly.

Around them, the rain had slowed to an almost intimate rhythmic patter. Lucy shivered as a cool breeze slid past. She pulled the blanket closer and stared out into the night.

"They died together in a motor vehicle accident.

We were driving through the mountains in Colorado. A boulder broke loose. They said it was the result of a heavy spring runoff. It crashed the front of the car. Travis and Emma and I were trapped in the back."

Jack inhaled sharply. "I'm so sorry, Lucy."

"Stuff happens." She swallowed hard, focusing on a tiny chip of paint on the arm of the chair.

"Yeah, it does."

"Their deaths were just as painful as being separated from Travis and Emma. That's why this ranch is so important. I got a second chance. Giving kids a second chance is what we're called to do. It's a huge responsibility that I can't afford to mess up."

"Lucy, believe it or not, I do get that. I'm not immune to what you're trying to do, and believe it or not, I understand second chances."

She nodded slowly, wanting to believe him.

Jack tucked his hands in his pockets. "So, the house. You never did explain where it came from.

"The house is not part of Big Heart Ranch."

"Is there something you're hiding?"

"Not at all." She released a breath. "I was engaged. We built this house. The engagement didn't work out, and I bought my portion of the house from him." There. Now he had it. Her pitiful story.

"I'm sorry it didn't work out."

"It was a long time ago."

He frowned and looked at her. "You're still

emotionally attached to the property, aren't you? Maybe you have hopes for reconciliation."

"Hardly," she scoffed. "He's moved on. Married a woman who doesn't come with baggage and sixty children." Lucy paused, realizing that her words were true. She had moved on. The pain that usually clawed at her chest when she thought of her former fiancé was gone.

When had that happened? How had she not noticed?

"The ranch? That was the problem?"

"Come on, Jack. Not many men want to marry a woman with a houseful of kids. Or in my case, a ranch-full."

"You do bring new meaning to the terms baggage and married to the job." He chuckled.

"I'm glad you find my pain so amusing."

"Aw, come on. If you don't laugh, what else can you do? Trust me, you aren't the only one who's been dumped."

"Not you? Big New York attorney?" She paused. "Let me guess. Supermodel?"

He straightened, looking almost offended. "How'd you know that?"

She laughed. "Because you're Captain Obvious."

"I like to think of myself as an open book."

Lucy choked on a laugh. "So why did you split up? Her ego was bigger than yours?"

"No. My bank account wasn't big enough."

"Ouch. That had to hurt."

"Surprisingly, not as much as I would have thought. We'd been lingering in the nowhere zone for so long, I didn't realize the relationship was dead until she'd been gone for two weeks and I hadn't even noticed."

Lucy looked up at Jack. She would have never guessed that his heart had suffered the same pain as hers. That didn't make them kindred spirits, though, she reminded herself.

Jack had buried his heartache, looking for all the world unscathed as he put on his lawyer face each day.

If only she could be so emotionless.

She shifted and tucked her feet beneath her. "Okay, this is getting far too maudlin for me. Can we change the subject?"

"Sure. How about food? I'm hungry."

"Didn't you eat s'mores?"

"Are you kidding? Those kids scarfed them down so fast, I would have lost fingers if I got between them and their appetites."

"The cook locks everything up at night."

"There isn't a single snack in this place?"

Lucy hesitated. "Well…" She met his gaze. "I do have my own personal locked closet downstairs in the pantry. I'm sure there's something in there. Whether it's edible or not is the real question."

He smiled. "Got the key with you?"

"I do." She folded up her blanket and stood, moving to the door. "Come on. But be quiet."

Jack held the door and followed Lucy through the entry and down the hall to the kitchen. He nearly knocked her over when she stopped in the middle of the room.

"Jack!" she hissed as he stumbled. "You're supposed to be quiet."

"I'm sorry. Why did you stop?"

"Because this is the closet." Lucy nodded to a tall door and pulled keys from her pocket. After fitting one into the lock, she turned to him. "I can't turn on the light until the door is closed. No one must see the inside of this closet."

He narrowed his eyes. "What sort of contraband do you have in there?"

The hardware creaked when she eased the door open.

"Come on," Lucy whispered.

When he didn't move, she grabbed his shirt and yanked him into the darkness before closing the door behind them.

The space was tight and she could sense when Jack turned slightly, as if trying to orient himself in the shadowed space. When the light came on, he blinked, shielding his eyes with a hand. He stepped back and knocked into her shoulder with his arm. "Sorry."

Lucy froze, caught in his gaze. His dark eyes widened, as he stared at her. Could he hear her heart beating out of control? She inched away, her back against the shelves.

This was a very bad idea. What was she thinking? How long had it been since she'd been this aware of a man? Too long. Why did it have to be this man?

Jack stared at her, and then his gaze slowly moved to the shelves behind her. The moment between them disappeared as his lips parted in amazement.

Lucy waited for the inevitable.

"Whoa. What is all this?" he said.

"Shh." She cringed and faced the shelves for the first time in three years. It was exactly as she'd feared. Nothing had changed. Every single space from top to bottom had been claimed. Even the floor was knee-deep in boxes.

Suddenly she saw everything through Jack's eyes, and humiliation slammed into her. Heart hammering, Lucy leaned over to catch her breath. "I didn't know what to do with everything when we called it off."

"Are you all right?" Jack asked. "You're hyperventilating."

She took a deep breath, closed her eyes and nodded.

"Are these wedding gifts?" he murmured.

"No. I returned all the gifts, along with apology notes."

"Then what is this stuff?"

"I'd been collecting things for months in preparation for…for our life. Our future together."

He eyed the appliances, towels, and blankets. "Why didn't you donate everything, or use it at the ranch?"

"Opening this closet was a reminder of my impaired judgment. It was easier to lock everything up and turn the key than deal with my issues."

"You haven't opened this door since then?"

"Correct."

Awkward silence fell between them.

Finally Jack brightened and opened his mouth. "You could always repurpose everything if you turn the lodge into…"

"Thank you, but no."

Jack stared at her. "Have you moved on or not?"

"I have." Lucy straightened.

"Great." He picked up a large package of chocolate bars, which had been tucked into a sealed Ziploc bag. "What's the expiration date on chocolate?"

"I don't know. Everything you see has been in here for three years."

"Three years!" His eyes widened. "What was this chocolate for?"

"Favors. They're engraved with our initials."

Jack inspected the fancy monograms on the

silver and white wrappers. "Are you opposed to eating them?"

She stared at the bag in his hand and hesitated only a moment before responding. "White, milk or dark?"

"I'm a dark chocolate guy."

"That's my favorite, too."

He handed her the plastic sack. "I think you should be the one to open the bag."

Lucy stared at the chocolate for several moments before unzipping the top and offering him a bar.

Jack tore open the wrapper and took a tentative bite. "Pretty good." He frowned. "I take that back. This is amazing chocolate."

Lucy bit into hers, releasing a flood gate of tamped-down memories and emotions. She chewed and swallowed, savoring the rich flavor. "Of course it is," she said to Jack. "Did you read that label? Imported from Belgium. His mother insisted."

"Highbrow?"

"One hundred percent."

"What did he do for a living?"

"Attorney."

When uncontrolled laughter spilled from his mouth, Lucy slapped a hand over his lips. "Quiet."

Jack gently removed her hand. His eyes locked on hers, and his fingers gently stroked her palm.

Lucy shivered. He was saying something, but she lost her concentration as she stared at his lips.

"Lucy?"

"Hmm?"

"We're not all jerks, you know."

"No?" She tugged her hand from his.

"No."

She bowed her head and reached for a bag of candy-coated, button-shaped chocolate pieces.

"Those are engraved, too," he noted. "Nice font."

Lucy tore open a bag and shoved a handful into her mouth.

"Good?"

"Amazingly satisfying," she said around a mouthful. "I should have done this years ago."

"Thank you for the chocolate," Jack said.

"You're welcome." She met his gaze. "Thanks for listening, Jack."

"I'm honored you shared with me."

"I didn't really have an option. It was either spill my secret or let you think I'm a crazed hoarder. I knew that wouldn't bode well for you approving the donation to the ranch."

"Lucy, look, we may have started out on the wrong foot…" He paused.

"But…"

Jack opened his mouth as if searching for the words.

Lucy cupped a hand to her ear. "I do believe I hear the sound of a Plan B thudding to the ground."

"No. Lucy, come on. It's not like that at all. I'm recognizing that I may be of use here at the ranch."

"You mean besides investigating us for corruption?"

"That's not why I'm here. I'm the fiduciary duty guy. Every organization can use a little assistance with management and reevaluation of fund distribution. The ranch has been around for five years, right?"

She clutched the bag of chocolates in a death grip. "What are you saying, Jack?"

"I'm saying that I'd like you to consider restructuring Big Heart Ranch."

Her stomach began to revolt. "Please, tell me you aren't serious."

"I'm very serious."

Quickly swallowing, she handed him the keys and the bag of chocolate. "Lock up when you're done."

"Lucy…"

She held up a hand. "Jack, I thought I'd prepared for every possible disaster, but you've managed to pull the rug out from under me. For the first time in a very long time, I don't know what to say."

"You're making too much out of this. I'm talking about working together."

"You and me? Managing Big Heart Ranch?" she sputtered.

"For a time. Yeah. See, I knew you'd get it."

"No. I didn't say I get anything. In fact, I can't imagine why you'd want to take over my ranch."

"Take over? What would I do with a ranch full of kids? I can barely handle one kid without breaking out in a cold sweat and hives."

Lucy stifled a sound of aggravation as she tried to move around him. She didn't remember his shoulders being so wide.

"Lucy, wait, please. We're only talking. Discussion is healthy."

"I feel less than healthy at the moment. In fact, all this chocolate is making me somewhat nauseous. Please move."

"So that's it? One minute we're sharing chocolate and the next I'm gum on the bottom of your red boots?"

"Jack, I'm tired and my blood sugar level is now off the charts, so while I'm willing to concede that I may be blowing this out of proportion, the idea of you restructuring my ranch is not something I want to discuss in this particular closet."

"You're right. I apologize. We can discuss this next week. I'm sure everything will look much better on Monday."

"Somehow, I suspect everything will look exactly the same on Monday," Lucy muttered as she walked out the door. She'd opened her heart and talked about her past for the first time in three years, and in return, Jack Harris had used her moment of weakness to betray her.

Maybe he was right; she did always prepare for the worst-case scenario—and this was exactly why.

# Chapter Eight

Jack knocked on the open office door and peeked in. Lucy's sister had her head buried in paperwork, but it was obvious even with her head down that Emma Maxwell was a slightly taller version of Lucy, with long dark hair.

He knocked again. "Excuse me? I'm looking for Lucy."

The petite brunette's head popped up. She smiled and quickly stood. "You must be Mr. Harris. Our new volunteer." She offered a conspiratorial wink.

Jack approached the desk and held out a hand. "Jack. And you're Emma?"

"Yes. Delighted to meet you. How's your aunt?"

"Doing well, I think. She's been mysteriously difficult to locate since she sent me out to the ranch."

Emma laughed.

"Is your sister around?" he asked.

"Lucy should be in anytime now. She did leave me a message to pass along to you." Emma reached for a notepad. "Ice cream around six tonight." She looked up. "Will that work for you?"

"It might. If I had my phone to check my schedule."

"She confiscated your phone?" Emma nearly choked on a laugh.

"Yeah, I tried to reach her all weekend on the bunkhouse phone without any response."

"Off the grid, no doubt, after I insisted she go home. That must have been some trail ride. Lucy looked like she was run over by a Mack Truck that backed up after to finish the job."

He smiled at the colorful yet oddly accurate description. "I'm a little surprised she went home without an argument. I haven't known your sister long, but it's pretty clear that she prefers to be the one giving orders."

"That's our Lucy." Emma glanced at the wall clock. "Do you want me to try to reach her? She's probably caught in traffic, but she'll have her Bluetooth on."

"Traffic? Where could there possibly be traffic around here?"

"Downtown Timber gets downright busy on senior discount day at the Piggly Wiggly."

"I hadn't considered that. I'll try back later today." He frowned. "Or maybe not. I have a chore list a mile long."

"Not that long, surely."

"Are you kidding? I'm Leo's replacement, and everyone tells me that Leo did the work of six men." He offered a wink.

Emma chuckled in return. "That might be a slight exaggeration."

"I'm beginning to think not." He glanced at his wrist where his watch used to be. "Do you suppose Lucy would mind if I used her desk to make a few quick calls? I'm researching a project for her."

"Jack, as far as I'm concerned, you can do whatever you like. If you'd be more comfortable, there's a small conference room down the hall, as well."

"Does that mean you aren't upset about the holdup of funds from the foundation?"

"I've heard all sorts of good things about you from General Butterfield. So, no, I'm no longer concerned."

"You're much more laid-back than your sister."

"Youngest child syndrome. And mostly everyone is more laid-back than my sister."

"Tell me, what do you think about the lodge?" Jack asked in an effort to gauge her reaction.

"It's a sad story isn't it?"

"Yeah. Too bad we can't turn things around and make it a functional part of the ranch."

"Lucy's broken engagement?"

"No. I'm talking about Big Heart Ranch Retreat Center." He smiled. "That's my working name for the project."

"Okay, now you have my curiosity."

"Picture a hewn wood entrance arch with the name branded across the top in dark letters." Jack gestured with his hands. "Can you see that?"

Emma's eyes lit up. "Yes. Yes, I can. Tell me more."

"I'm still working on the details, but I'm thinking combination vacation rental, event venue and guest ranch. The bottom line is a solid income stream for the ranch."

"That's a fantastic idea. What did Lucy think?"

Jack grimaced. "Your sister wasn't as enthusiastic as you are, which is why I'm working on a full presentation."

"Shot you down, huh?"

Jack nodded. "Faster than I could say 'think about it.' For some reason she's taking my idea as a personal attack. I'm in awe of what Lucy does around here. My ideas for that house would make her life easier."

"Lucy doesn't handle change well."

"I noticed."

"You have to remember that she's a lot like Dub. She's had responsibility on her shoulders all her life. Lucy never really got to be a kid. The only thing that ensures she can sleep at night is being in control."

He tilted his head, considering Emma's words. "Any thoughts on how I can get Lucy on board?"

"Try to understand that you've terrified her, Jack. However, there is hope. I have learned over the years that it's always best to present ideas in layers. Give Lucy time to wrap her head around the idea first."

"You certainly know your sister."

"Yes. I do."

"So what do you suggest?"

"It depends on you. Travis and I have different approaches. I move slowly, like I'm trying to gentle an anxious mare. Travis gallops ahead, does what he wants and apologizes later. He'd rather ask for pardon than permission. Both are surprisingly effective techniques. It simply depends on how much time you have."

He pondered Emma's words for a moment, understanding dawning as he recalled the terror in her eyes when he'd suggested restructuring the ranch. How could he get Lucy to understand he wasn't threatening her control, but trying to ease her burden?

Jack turned at the sound of labored breathing behind him. A portly gentleman in a white short-sleeved dress shirt and mud-brown trousers, and with a faux-leather briefcase, filled the doorway, pausing to catch his breath.

"Mr. Fillister," Emma said. "I didn't realize you have an appointment with Lucy?"

"Woo-ee. Hot out there. I'm sweating like a politician on election day." He wiped his brow with a rumpled handkerchief. "Lucy's not around?"

"Not at the moment."

"We didn't officially have an appointment. I wanted her to review the new contracts for the office supplies and equipment."

"I can do that," Jack said without thinking.

Emma stared at him, eyes wide.

"Would that be okay?" Jack continued. "I mean, it *is* what I do for a living. Contract law."

"Go ahead, Jack. Lucy should be along any moment, anyhow."

The salesman frowned as he assessed Jack. "I don't think we've met, sir."

"Jackson Harris. I'm helping out at the ranch this summer."

"I can tell you ain't from around here," the man drawled.

"How can you tell?"

"That accent is a dead giveaway."

"*I* have an accent?"

"Shore do."

"Huh. I had no idea." Jack offered a hand, which was accepted.

"Fred Fillister. Fillister World-Renowned Office Supply, Timber, Oklahoma."

"World-renowned?"

Fred laughed. "In this part of the world, we like to say."

Jack couldn't help but laugh, too. "I like that, Fred."

"Why don't I show you gentlemen to the conference room?" Emma offered.

It was less than thirty minutes before a door slammed in the building, followed by muttering and the rapid shuffling of feet outside the conference room. Lucy Maxwell had no doubt arrived. A moment later, the conference room door opened.

She stood with one hand on the knob. With the other she pushed her bangs off her face. "Mr. Fillister, I'm so sorry I was away from my desk." Her gaze took in the papers strewn across the table, the empty coffee cups and the box of doughnuts, and her eyes widened a fraction. Her jaw tightened. "Did we have an appointment? How may I assist you?"

"Actually, your attorney has taken care of everything."

"My attorney?" Lucy's gaze chilled as it slid from the salesman to him.

Fred Fillister tilted his head as he assessed her. "Are you all right, Lucy? You look like you haven't slept in a few days."

She moved into the room and smiled brightly. Too brightly. "I'm fine. Wonderful." She glanced at the papers on the table again. "What's all this?"

"I brought those contracts for the office supplies and copiers."

Jack cleared his throat. "I've been reviewing the contracts with Fred here."

"Oh?" Her left eye twitched.

"We agreed that Fillister World-Renowned Office Supplies can do better."

"A better deal. From Fred?" Lucy swallowed.

"Yes. He's going to increase the discount and throw in an extended warranty."

Her eyes rounded. "That sounds excellent."

Jack smiled. "Fred and I thought so. He understands that while you want to support local businesses, this is a competitive market."

"Yes. Definitely," Lucy agreed.

"I'll get those contracts updated and stop by next week," Fred added as he stood and brushed doughnut crumbs from his shirt. He pointed his index finger at Jack. "Front and center on the webpage?"

"Right there with our other valuable donors."

Fred grinned. "'Preciate it, Jack."

"Thanks, Mr. Fillister," Lucy chirped as the salesman waddled down the hall. She turned to Jack once their guest was out of earshot. "Front and center on the webpage?"

"Is that an issue for your web guy?"

"It will be, if you promise front and center to all our vendors. And by the way, meet the web guy."

"Why am I not surprised?"

Lucy crossed her arms, and he waited for what was coming. The dark eyes sparked with thunder and lightning. A storm was about to hit.

"Look, Jack, while I'm very grateful, and actually stunned that you got Fred to budge, I have to ask, what do you think you're doing?"

"There is no nefarious plan brewing, Lucy."

She eyed him with doubt.

"You weren't here and I was. I'm good at negotiation. I can be very persuasive."

"I'll remember that." She began to clean up the table.

Jack reached out to stop her. When their hands collided, she drew back. "You shouldn't be cleaning up," he said. "Don't you have an assistant?"

"Assistant what?"

"You know, a secretary, clerk, personal admin. Someone who can prepare a conference room for meetings, and then go out for doughnuts."

Lucy stepped around him and closed the doughnut box.

"Who got the doughnuts?" she asked.

"Emma."

Jack picked up the trash can and brought it to the table. "Lucy, you're running an organization. It's efficient to have an assistant. Perhaps one with basic web skills."

"We're family here, Jack. Travis or my sister are happy to help me when I need assistance."

"Would that be your sister with the sign on her door that says Children's Therapist and Child Care Director? The one with the two babies in her office, who also runs some company called Range-Pro?"

"Assistants cost money." She stopped and stared at him. "You're the one causing the cash flow issues."

"That's not exactly correct. My job is to be sure Big Heart Ranch is utilizing the funds from the Brisbane Foundation in a fiduciary manner."

She offered a dramatic sigh. "Life was much simpler when your only agenda item was to prove I'm a lowlife crook, preying on the elderly."

"That might have been somewhat true last Monday, but six hours in a saddle and seventy-two hours on the trail have persuaded me that the bigger problem here is the allocation of resources."

"Speak for yourself, Jack. You may have a problem, but we do not. This is my business and I have been running the ranch for five years without your fiduciary duty."

"All the same. Brisbane Foundation sent me here. You and my aunt decided it would be six weeks. So I plan to share my thoughts with you until my time here is complete."

"Great," Lucy muttered. "Just terrific!"

He stepped back and looked at Lucy. Really looked at her. Besides the bruised chin from the ball game, she had dark circles under her eyes and the sparkle was missing from her gaze.

"Are you feeling okay?" he asked.

"Why does everyone keep asking me that?"

"Maybe because you look a little rough, and as I heard often enough on the trail, you act like you have a burr under your saddle. Have you considered taking the day off?"

"Thanks. I appreciate the ego boost, but I can't stay home and leave everything to Emma again."

"If you had an admin, you could."

"Way to hammer home your point, counselor,"

she said. "If you'll excuse me, I have a job to do."
Lucy swept from the room and started down the
hall.

He followed. "You said I could shadow you."

"Today might not be the best day."

"Fair enough. How about later in the week?"

"Sure. I'll let you know this evening. Okay?"

"That works, but may I have my phone and
watch back in the meantime?"

She stopped and turned, her face becoming red.
"Didn't I return them?"

"No."

"You went the entire weekend without your
phone and watch?" Lucy sighed. "I'm really
sorry." A frown crossed her face. "Let me check
my saddle bag. It's in my office."

"It was actually sort of liberating to go off the
grid. I hear you do it often."

"Not often, but on occasion. I have a lot of
things crowding my mind here at the ranch. Sometimes God and I need to be alone."

Jack stepped closer. Close enough to see the
weariness that rode on her shoulders. "You do
too much."

"Excuse me?" Attitude and annoyance began
a slow stampede across her face.

"You've got to start delegating, or you're going
to burn out. Trust me. I know."

"At the risk of sounding harsh, Jack, I might be
able to delegate if the Brisbane Foundation fund-

ing comes through. Right now I'm on a tightrope, trying to pull a Plan B out of my hat while balancing the funds we do have."

"Lucy, with or without budget approval, you aren't going to change your management style unless you're pushed. Consider this me pushing."

"What exactly is my management style?"

He hesitated, rubbing his chin. "You do lean toward micromanagement."

Her eyes rounded, and Jack checked for smoke coming out of her ears. He waited for the backlash.

Instead of responding, she started walking again.

"Lucy?"

"Let me get you your electronics, Mr. Harris."

Uh-oh. They were back to Mr. Harris.

Jack followed her down the hall to an office that would have terrified a lesser man. His gaze took in the haphazard stacks of paperwork and books. He was fairly certain that there was a desk somewhere under the various piles. An ivy plant in a colorful porcelain Western boot sat on the window ledge begging for water.

"Did you file a police report?" he asked.

"What?" Lucy sputtered.

"Someone ransacked your office."

"Funny, Harris."

"This is a pretty small office for the ranch director," he observed.

"I don't need much room to micromanage," she returned.

They faced off across her desk. All five feet two inches of Lucy Maxwell stared him down. What was it about this particular woman that made him want to protect her and kiss her at the same time? She was as stubborn as he was, and therein was the irony. He'd rather argue with Lucy than spend time with anyone else.

"So I'll see you tonight?" he murmured.

Lucy blinked. "What?"

"Tonight. Ice cream. It's a date?"

Pink tinged her cheeks. "Ice cream, yes. Date? Hardly."

"Maybe you and I should go to dinner sometime," he suggested.

Her mouth opened but nothing came out. Flustered again.

Jack turned with a smile, realizing he should leave while he was ahead. For once. "See you at six, Lucy."

"For the record, Lucy, I think Jack is adorbs," Emma said as she sorted the stack of mail in her hands.

Lucy nearly choked on her coffee. Clearing a place among the paperwork, she cautiously set the mug down on her desk before pinning her sister with a pointed gaze. "Adorbs? What are you? Sixteen?"

"No, but I hang out with adolescents all day." Emma sighed. "I need to get out more. You and Travis and Tripp are the only grown-ups I ever see, and Tripp doesn't talk."

"You've been a single mom too long. It wouldn't hurt for you to get a sitter on occasion and have a mental health day. Have lunch with friends. Go to a movie."

"You're giving me social life advice? You haven't gone to lunch with a friend in years and a date, well, not since…you know," Emma said as she placed the stack of mail on Lucy's desk.

"I'm going out…" She glanced at her watch. "In fifteen minutes, as it so happens."

"With three five-year-old escorts. Not exactly my idea of a hot date."

"Who would I go on a hot date with?"

Emma raised a hand. "Hello. Are you paying attention? Jack, of course. Minus the triplets." She looked Lucy up and down. "Is that what you're wearing?"

Lucy glanced down at her sundress and boots. "What's wrong with this?"

"There's a new dress shop in Timber. You could get some serious clothes. After all, this is Jack Harris we're talking about. The man is the whole package. Tall, dark and handsome. If you made an effort, he might ask you out. Alone, I mean."

Lucy's thoughts tumbled to the man who only

hours before had stood at her desk, leaving her speechless when he'd made the very same suggestion. "Jack?" she repeated.

"Yes. Jack." She started checking off on her fingers. "He's smart. Doesn't live with his parents. Is gainfully employed and doesn't play video games all day."

"While that is all true, Jack and I have nothing in common."

"You're wrong, Lucy. You and Jack are so much alike it's almost scary."

Lucy paused. She quickly shook her head, discarding the possible truth of her sister's words.

"Everything he said tells me that the man genuinely respects you and cares about you."

"You and Jack discussed me?" Her voice raised an octave.

"It wasn't like that. We were discussing the ranch."

Lucy blew a raspberry. "The ranch. Yes. The truth is Jack Harris only cares about taking control of the ranch."

"That's not true. He's an attorney. The man has more options than Italian loafers. Why would he want our ranch?"

"I haven't figured that part out yet, but I will." She fingered the stacks of paper on her desk. "Did you give me my messages?"

Emma reached in her back pocket and handed over a neat wad of pink memo notes.

"That's a lot of memos. I was only gone three days."

"The budget hasn't been approved. Checks are delayed. Contracts haven't been signed. Everyone wants to know what's going on."

"You know what's going on. Jack Harris."

"Yes. I know, and I get it, but you haven't told anyone else but me and Travis. Maybe you should."

Lucy flipped through the papers one by one. "We ran out of supplies for VBS? Order them. Overnight, if necessary. You don't need my approval for that."

"With the state of the budget, I've been afraid to do anything. And Travis is no help. I mention finances and he suddenly has chores to do. In a pasture, without cell service."

Micromanager. Jack's words slapped her in the face.

Emma and Travis did whatever she told them to. They waited for her to lead them. Maybe it was time to delegate more than ordering doughnuts and answering her phone.

Jack might be right. Her stomach churned at the thought.

"I'm sorry, Em," she murmured. "Thank you for handling things while I was gone."

"Not a problem." Emma picked dead leaves

from the pathetic ivy in Lucy's window. "What did you do to this plant?"

"Nothing. I bought it because the lady said you can't kill ivy."

"And yet, you seem to have proven that theory wrong."

Lucy grabbed a bottle of water from her tote and moved to the window. "Did he mention the lodge?" she asked.

"Jack?"

"Who else?"

"He might have."

"I rest my case."

"At least give his idea a chance," Emma said. "You're dismissing him on principle."

"That's not true." Lucy frowned as she carefully released a stream of water into the plant pot.

"Stop," Emma said, grabbing her wrist. "That plant needs a drink of water. Don't drown the sucker."

Lucy plunked the bottle on the windowsill and turned to Emma, hands on hips. "Admit it. I'm a terrible director, aren't I?"

"Whoa, where did that come from? You're a business school graduate. You're a Godly woman, inside and out. And you love these kids."

"Too much. Maybe this ranch needs someone with a calculator heart like Jack's instead of…" She swept her hand around the room. "An unorganized mess."

"Where is this coming from?"

"Jack, that's where."

"Give yourself a break, would you? You've been under a lot of stress lately. Maybe you need a vacation."

Lucy stared out the window at the ranch she loved, her gaze taking in the little chapel across the way, surrounded by redbuds and a huge magnolia. "Or maybe it's time I stopped fooling myself."

The administration building's front glass doors closed with a bang, and both sisters swung around in time to see Jack in the doorway.

Lucy glanced at the clock, almost expecting to hear the tolling of the executioner's bell as the clock struck six.

"Oh, look, here's Mr. Adorbs now," Emma whispered.

Lucy elbowed her. "Stop that."

He glanced at both sisters. "Everything okay? Did I dress appropriately?"

"You're fine," Lucy said, taking in his tan chinos and open-neck blue cotton shirt. The man's annoyance factor failed to distract from his good looks.

"Better than fine, Jack," Emma gushed, taking the words Lucy would never dare utter right out of her mouth.

"Thank you. How about you, Lucy? How are you feeling?"

"Okay. That's it." Her glance slowly swept over Jack and Emma. "No one is to ask another question about my health, mental or otherwise. Got it?"

Emma nodded.

"I guess that means you're feeling fine," Jack said.

"You guessed right. Now you and I have an appointment with triplets. We promised, and you know my thoughts on that. The girls and Dub will be waiting for us at the meeting hall." She turned on her boot heel and headed outside, with Jack a step behind.

"Have fun, you two," Emma called out. "Stay out as late as you like."

"Remind me to fire her when we get back," Lucy said.

"Can you fire your own sister?"

"I can try."

Jack laughed. "You're fortunate to have Emma."

Lucy grumbled in response as they walked along the sidewalk.

"I've got my car parked behind your admin building," he said.

"Are you still renting a car?" she asked. "Isn't that sort of expensive?"

"Cost of doing business."

"Nice for you. We'll take my car. I know where the place is. I'll drive." She glanced over at him, taking in the expression on his face. "You have a problem with me driving?"

"Not at all, I'm just a little concerned about your vehicle. Old Yeller."

"Old Yeller?"

"Yeah, that mustard-colored car of yours. It's like a Labrador retriever who's overdue for doggie retirement."

"Jack, don't spare my feelings. Tell me how you really feel."

"You're the ranch director. You deserve a respectable vehicle."

"I don't spend ranch funds on my personal needs."

"Lucy, a decent car is part of doing business. It's not a luxury, it's a necessity. You shouldn't drive potential donors around the ranch in that old jalopy. You're the director. That requires you play the part."

"My car isn't that old."

"Not old? It appears quite, uh, vintage to me."

"Vintage. Not even close. If you want to talk vintage, let me tell you about my father's truck. He had a wonderful red hump-backed Chevy pickup. He'd take us for ice cream once a week in that truck. Thinking about that Chevy reminds me how much I miss him, and miss those times as a family."

"I'm sorry, Lucy."

"It's all right. Good memories last forever, you know."

"Do they?" He raised a brow. "So what happened to the pickup?"

"Who knows? A lot of things disappeared after my parents died. Until my cousin finally showed up, it was assumed we didn't have any living relatives."

"That's too bad."

Lucy nodded.

"How old is it? Your car?" he asked.

"The Honda? Eighteen years."

"Eighteen! Good grief. That car is over one hundred and twenty in dog years."

Lucy stopped and stared at him. She burst out laughing at the absurdity of his comment. Moisture blurred her vision as she kept laughing. Finally, she cleared her throat and held out a hand. "Okay. You win. You can drive."

"My car?"

"Yes. Only because I'm afraid I'll spontaneously start laughing if we take mine, and that might be hazardous on the road."

"Thank you." He smiled.

"You won't be smiling when there are kids' fingerprints and other unidentifiable residue all over your pristine vehicle."

"Residue?"

"Uh-huh. Kids pick up anything and everything. Then they shove it in their pockets or in their noses. It always winds up on your windows, or smashed on the floor mats."

He stared at her for a moment, mouth slightly ajar with horror.

When they reached the chow hall, Jack held open the glass door. A pleasant-looking middle-aged woman waited for them just inside.

"Lorna, you remember Jack Harris from the trail ride?" Lucy asked.

"Oh, yes. The catcher who couldn't decide which team he was on."

Jack grimaced.

"Where are the kids?" Lucy asked.

"The girls are using the restroom one last time."

"How've they been?" Lucy asked.

"Good. The girls are so envious of Dub's snake-skin and blue ribbon. They can't wait to meet his buddy."

Lucy looked past Lorna to a table where Dub sat, swinging his legs back and forth and fiddling with the buttons of his shirt.

Lorna followed her gaze. "That boy is so excited."

"Anxious, too," Lucy added.

"Excuse me, ladies," Jack murmured. He walked to where Dub sat clenching and unclenching his hand.

Dub's face lit up with obvious relief when he saw Jack. Her breath caught as the little boy gazed up at Jack with his heart in his eyes.

"You came," he breathed, eyes wide.

"I said I would," Jack said quietly.

Lucy blinked, swallowing past the lump of emotion in her throat. She knew what it was like to be disappointed over and over again. Little Dub would never go through that again if she had her way.

"Yeth, you did." Dub nodded. "My sisters are here."

"Good. I want to meet them."

Two replicas of Dub came out of the restroom. They looked like girly girls, with flyaway, fine blond hair held back with headbands. One wore a white headband, the other pink. It was obviously the only way to identify the girls, as they were mirror images, down to their pink tops and patterned pink shorts. They smiled, revealing that they too were missing their front teeth like their brother.

Jack offered an exaggerated bow. "Ladies, I'm Dub's buddy, Mr. Jack. Pleased to meet you."

Both girls giggled.

"Can you guess which one is Ann and which one is Eva?" Lucy asked from behind him.

"I can't. They look like identical princesses to me," he said.

Pleased smiles lifted the girls' lips.

"Ann always wears the white headband," Dub said.

"Ann," Jack said. He turned to the other little girl. "Eva," he said with a grin.

Lucy's heart melted as the little girls soaked in

the special attention. Every little girl should have a daddy who made them feel like a princess.

"You okay?" Jack murmured as he turned toward her. His warm breath tickled her neck.

"Yes. Yes. Of course."

"Ready to go?" he asked.

"Yes. We're ready. Right?" Lucy asked, her glance taking in the triplets.

All three nodded.

"Mr. Jack is driving today."

A worried frown crossed Dub's face. "Do you know how to get to the ice cream store?"

"My car can find anything." He took Dub's hand. "Come on. I'll show you. It talks."

"Cars can't talk." Dub laughed.

"Not every car. But mine sure can."

Dub's eyes rounded and he looked at his sisters, wiggling his eyebrows up and down.

"Stooping to cheap party tricks to win them over?" Lucy whispered.

"Absolutely. Whatever it takes," Jack returned. "I have no shame."

"Finally. Something we can agree on."

# Chapter Nine

"This was a lot more fun than I anticipated," Jack said. His gaze followed the triplets, whose laughter was unleashed like a kite tail as they raced around the gravel playground.

"I'm guessing your expectations were quite low."

"Gloating is not an attractive trait, Lucy."

She chuckled as she bit into her cone, releasing melted vanilla ice cream onto her chin.

He grinned as she struggled to catch the drips that ran leisurely over her fingers.

"You can stop laughing and hand over the napkins."

He offered a stack of napkins.

"You and the kids shoveled in a lot of ice cream and toppings in a very short amount of time. In fact, I'm pretty sure your sundae was mostly chocolate sauce."

He leaned back against the bench. "Shoveling in ice cream like a kid. I haven't done that in a long time."

"No? You caught right on, like an old pro."

"Which is why I am recovering on a bench, while they run around," Jack said. He turned to Lucy. "The park was an excellent idea."

"If you feed kids sugary treats, you have to let them run it off. That's rule eighty-six."

"Right after 'don't break promises'?"

"No. 'Don't break promises' is near the top."

"Exactly how many rules are there?"

She shook her head as she seemed to consider his question. "Too many to count."

Jack stretched his arm along the back of the bench, accidently touching Lucy's warm shoulder. For once she didn't move away, and he allowed himself to pretend that she welcomed his touch.

"Excuse me?" a voice said from behind the bench.

Jack and Lucy both turned to see an elderly couple standing behind them, with a beagle on a leash. Jack stood, as did Lucy. "Yes, ma'am?" he asked.

"Your children are simply adorable. And so well behaved."

"They—" Lucy began.

Jack interrupted. He put an arm around her shoulder and pulled her close. "Thank you so much."

"You certainly are blessed," the woman added.

"That we are," Jack said.

"Would it be all right if our little pup said hello to them? He so loves children, and he never bites."

"Of course." He took Lucy's hand and they followed the couple to the triplets. Once again, Lucy didn't resist.

"What are you doing?" she whispered.

"Let's not disappoint them."

Dub, Ann and Eva petted the little dog for several minutes. As the couple walked away, Dub raced to Jack.

"Jack! Jack! That man thinks you're my dad."

"He does?"

A small wistful smile settled on Dub's lips. He looked up at Jack. "I wish you were my dad, Jack. I do."

"Thank you, Dub. That's the nicest thing anyone's ever said to me."

Dub raced back to his sister, and Jack's gaze followed. Worrisome thoughts nipped at him. He turned to Lucy and reluctantly released her hand.

"What will happen to Dub and his sisters at the end of summer?" he asked.

"They'll go back into foster care." She glanced away, her expression solemn.

"Separate homes?" A knot twisted his gut.

"Once they leave the ranch, it's out of my hands. Of course, the ideal scenario is one home, but the likelihood of that is slim."

"Have you ever thought about taking them in permanently?"

"Me?" Stunned surprise crossed Lucy's face as her eyes connected with his. "You mean fostering them?" Her eyes widened with alarm.

"Or adopting. You've obviously got what it takes."

"I do?"

"Hold that thought," he said, while pulling a ringing cell from his pocket. His aunt.

"Sure, Aunt Meri. Not a problem."

"Everything okay?" Lucy asked when he ended the call.

"She asked me to swing by," Jack said.

"I can call Travis to pick us up."

"No. This won't take long. She'd love to see Dub. I've told her about him."

"You told your aunt about Dub Lewis?"

"Sure. Why not? He's my buddy."

"I thought you were allergic to kids, Jack."

He shrugged, unable to explain what he didn't understand himself, that Dub had wormed his way into his heart and even cured him of kid-itis.

The time spent with Dub had begun to ease the crushing pain of Daniel's death, as well.

Lucy slowly shook her head. "Jack, you never cease to amaze me. Whenever I think I have you pigeonholed, I'm either pleasantly surprised or totally annoyed."

"I like to keep you on your toes." He winked. "You might want to wipe that ice cream off your nose before we leave."

She groaned. "Why didn't you tell me?"

"I just did."

She ineffectively swiped at her nose and looked to him for approval.

"Missed it by a mile." Jack leaned forward, the pad of his finger touching the tip of her nose.

His gaze rested on her lips, and for a moment he silently debated eliminating the space between them. He took a deep breath and moved away.

"Am I okay?" she asked.

"Lucy, you are more than okay," he said softly. "In fact, once I convince you to repurpose the lodge, you'll be perfect."

"Things are going so nicely today. Don't start." Lucy stood. "I'll get the kids into the car."

When they pulled up to the large, circular drive outside the Brisbane estate, Jack parked beneath the shade of a big magnolia near a small fountain.

Dub and his sisters unbuckled their seat belts and scrambled out of the car to stare at the water bubbling over a mermaid sculpture perched on the edge of the fountain.

"Are you sure your aunt is okay with this?" Lucy asked quietly as they approached the front door. She nodded toward the children.

Jack shot her a curious glance. "Why wouldn't she be?"

"There's five of us. We're like a…"

"A family?"

Her eyes rounded. "I was going to say a troupe."

"She'll love our troupe," he said.

"Look. Bunnies," Dub said.

Near the front door, the children crouched down to examine a concrete lawn ornament nestled in the grass. The figurines depicted a family of bunnies.

Jack pressed the bell, and a shadow appeared

behind the stained glass panels. A young woman opened the door.

"Come in. Mrs. Brisbane is on her way. Hello again, Mr. Harris. Good afternoon, ma'am." She held out a hand for Lucy. "I'm Estelle, her personal assistant."

"Nice to meet you," Lucy said.

With gentle hands on the children's backs, Lucy led them into the house. The little faces turned upward to stare at the ornate crystal chandelier.

The soft tap of Meredith's cane on the marble floor preceded Jack's aunt into the large entry hall.

A smile lit up his aunt's face as she eyed the children standing behind Lucy. "Who do we have here?"

"Dub, Eva and Ann," Jack said.

"Triplets. They're adorable. Please, do come in."

"Kids, this is my aunt, Mrs. Brisbane."

"Oh, please, they may call me Aunt Meri." Her face warmed with pleasure at the trio.

"Aunt Meri, what was it you wanted to see me about?" Jack asked. "Is everything okay?"

"Let's move to the solarium. The children might enjoy my fish."

Dub's ears perked. "Fish?"

"Yes. I have a giant aquarium. Follow Miss Estelle. She'll take you right to them. I'm a little slow, but I'll be along."

Once the children were busy observing the

large tank, Meredith ushered Jack and Lucy to a seat on the wicker divan. Large windows with crisp off-white Roman shades provided a view of the grounds, and though it was summer, air conditioning kept the room comfortable.

"I'm having a small soiree next weekend, Jackson, and I was hoping to persuade you to attend."

"You could have asked on the phone."

"True. However, I find my powers of persuasion function best in person."

"A soiree?" he asked.

"Yes. Lucy, you are of course invited, as well. Actually, this is quite providential." She smiled. "I had no idea that you and Jack…"

"Oh, no. Your nephew and I are not… I'm only here because…" She paused. "Jack is Dub's buddy for the summer. This was a promised outing." Lucy flashed him an appeal for assistance.

"Lucy didn't know if I could handle three kids, much less one, all by myself. She took pity on me."

"Nonetheless, Lucy dear, you would do well to get to know more members of the Timber community. Your ranch could only benefit. I've been singing your praises for years. Jackson will escort you."

Lucy's gaze skittered nervously to him and then away. "Um, thank you, Meredith. I'd love to attend."

"Was that all, Aunt Meri?"

"A few more things." She turned to her assistant, who stood near the tank talking to the children. "Estelle, dear, do you mind asking the chef to bring in lemonade?"

"Of course not, Mrs. Brisbane."

Meredith turned back to Jack. "That friend of mine in New York would like to talk to you about subletting your place."

Jack raised a brow and scratched his head. "Really?"

"Yes, and she mentioned a very nice price."

"I'm going to have to think about that."

"What is there to think about, Jackson? There's nothing in New York for you anymore."

"What about Dad?"

"Your father lives in hotels and is rarely in the same city long enough to call any place home. In fact, if you're here full-time, he might be encouraged to visit."

"I'm still going to have to think this over."

"Don't think too long." She pulled a card from her pocket. "Here's the phone number."

"Thanks, Aunt Meri." He fingered the card and put it in his back pocket.

"Now, about the stables." She glanced outside in the direction of the building that used to house the horses. "It's been empty for years. I've decided to lease the building and the yards."

"Good idea."

"Yes. Could you do a quick walk-through of

the building? Most everything has been boxed up. Take anything in there you want before I have a local charity haul the rest away."

"I can do that."

"Perhaps you could take Dub with you. I'd like to spend some quality time with the ladies, so we'll enjoy some lemonade and talk about you while you are gone."

Jack laughed. "Fair enough. Dub, would you like to go to the stables?"

"Yeth." The little boy rushed to follow them.

Meredith stood. "Let me locate those keys for you."

As they approached the front hall, his aunt pulled the keys from her pocket.

"I thought you had to find the keys."

"I wanted a chance to talk to you." She smiled. "I see you and Lucy are working together?"

He frowned. "Yes. But don't get any ideas. We're working. That's all."

"Does that mean you're going to release the donation documentation? It's already two weeks overdue. Lucy must be extremely stressed."

"I'm actually doing my best to take some pressure off Lucy."

"Oh? Why not approve the proposal and be done with it?"

"If I approve the funds, I won't have a reason to stay at the ranch."

"You want to stay? I'm a bit confused."

"Aunt Meri, it turns out you were right about the ranch."

"Aha! I told you so."

"Yes, you did. I have a few ideas to help Big Heart Ranch, and ultimately help Lucy, in a very big way. The problem is that she's a little set in her ways. The only leverage I have is that unsigned donation proposal."

"Jackson, you're playing with fire here. This cannot end well."

"I disagree. I'm giving my all to this project. To tell you the truth, Aunt Meri, for the first time in a very long time, I'm really enjoying myself and I'm excited about what I'm doing. I believe I'm contributing to something that will benefit Big Heart Ranch and the children and staff."

"I don't understand why you're taking the long route around instead of the direct route."

"Trust me, Aunt Meri, I know what I'm doing."

She placed a hand on his arm. "I hope so."

Jack kissed her cheek. "Come on, Dub, let's go exploring."

They walked outside across the drive and around the back of the house to the large stables complex.

"You gots horses, Mr. Jack?"

"Not anymore. We did when I was younger."

"Are you fixin' to get horses?"

"Sort of. My aunt is going to let someone else

keep their horses here." Jack unlocked the massive wooden door and pulled it open. Warm air rushed past them, struggling to get out.

"Wow, sure is a big stable," Dub said. "Bigger than the one at the ranch."

Their voices and footsteps echoed through the empty building.

"Hot, too." Jack strode through to the back and opened the double doors on the far end, to get the summer air circulating. Then he hit the switch to start the blades of the large overhead fans.

Beside him, Dub bent down and picked up something shiny on the ground. "Look. I found a quarter. Can I keep it?"

"It's yours."

Dub pointed overhead. "Is that your loft?"

Jack glanced up. "Yeah. It's dusty up there. You might want to wait down here."

"I wanna go with you."

"Okay, but hold that rail and be careful." The wood creaked as they mounted the dozen steps to the loft.

Dub sneezed. "This doesn't look like a loft. How come you don't have hay?"

"Because we don't need hay without horses."

"Oh, yeah." Dub nodded.

They both stared at the stacked and sheet-covered furniture that took up one entire wall, along with dusty boxes.

"Furniture?" Jack murmured.

"Lots of it," Dub said.

"Maybe enough to fill an empty house." He'd have to make sure his aunt didn't get rid of anything until he had more time to inventory what was here.

"Look, Mr. Jack. A bicycle. It has training wheels, too."

Jack turned and smiled at the sight. Propped against a spindle-legged chair was a red bicycle, complete with a bell and a basket. "That's my bicycle. See the baseball card in the spokes? I put that there."

"Cool. Can we take it downstairs?"

"Sure. But let's look around some more before we do that."

"I know how to ride," Dub announced.

"I bet you can."

"How old were you when you rode that bike?"

"I think I was your age. I got another bigger bike later, and this one was tucked away."

"Did your brother have a bike, too?"

"He did. I don't know where his bike is." Jack glanced around. Beneath a window, a large box with his name and one with Daniel's sat side by side. "Dub, can you sit on the floor for a few minutes while I check out these boxes? I might find something in there for you."

"Treasures?" Dub asked as he settled cross-legged on the floor.

"You never know. I can't remember what's inside."

Jack pushed open the small attic window before he, too, settled on the floor and tugged the box with his name toward him. He slid his hand under the flap.

"What is it?"

Jack pulled out hardbound childhood classics. "Books."

"My sissies read lots. Can we bring them books?"

"Sure." Jack pulled out a plastic bag filled with metal toy cars. "Look at this, Dub."

Dub clapped his hands. "Whoa. Cars. What are you going to do with them?"

"They're yours, if Miss Lucy says it's okay."

"She will. I know she will. Can we ask her?"

"Absolutely." He held the bag out to Dub. "Why don't you hold them for me?"

"Yes, sir, Mr. Jack." Delight spread like jam across Dub's freckled face.

"I want to look for…" Jack grinned as he pulled boots and a helmet from the box. "This is what I hoped we'd find. Boots. My old riding boots. You know what that means?"

"What?"

"You can ride Grace."

Dub's eyes lit up. "This has been a real good treasure hunt."

"It has." Jack reached for his brother's box, hating that he was going to look inside, but unable to stop himself. The box held bits of his brother's life and right now, at this moment, he needed to see those pieces.

He inched back one flap at a time. Toys. The letters DH had been written on the tag of a chocolate-brown chenille-stuffed bear. Lifting the toy to his face, he inhaled. How could that be? The soft fabric still smelled like Daniel.

Twenty-five years. How was it possible that in one breath he was nine years old again, having his heart torn from his chest once more?

Jack's jaw tightened as he gripped the toy. He swallowed hard, his eyes filling with emotion.

"Jack?"

He turned at Lucy's soft voice.

"Everything okay up here?" she asked from the top step to the attic.

"Yeth," Dub answered. "Look, Miss Lucy. I have cars. Mr. Jack says I can keep them if you say I can. Can I?"

"Sure, Dub. Let's take them downstairs."

"What about the bike?" Dub asked.

"I'll bring the bike downstairs and we can put it in the trunk of the car," Jack said. "Go with Miss Lucy, Dub. I'll be right there."

"Mr. Jack, I like it here. Your aunt is nice and I

like the fish, and the lemonade, too. Can we come back?" Dub asked quietly.

"Maybe." Lucy met his gaze and he sighed. "We will come back, Dub. I promise."

Jack sat where he was, staring out the small attic window at the tops of the peach trees in the orchard. Minutes later he heard footfalls on the steps again. "Jack, I can take the children to the ranch and come back for you later," Lucy said softly.

"No. I'm coming. I…" He faltered. "The heaviness in my heart I'm used to. This… I didn't expect this."

"Your brother?"

"Yeah. Funny. You think you have a tight lid on your emotions. Everything is under control, and then when you least expect it, you're blindsided."

She sat down on the floor next to him and took his hand. "I'm so very sorry, Jack."

He shrugged. "Why are you sorry?"

"I'm sorry because you're hurting."

She spoke with care, as though he were a child. And in a way, when it came to Daniel, he still was.

Lucy continued. "I understand grief. Maybe it's the one thing you and I have in common. It isn't just about loss. It's about the past, the future and the now. Grief touches everything in our lives."

Her petite hand clutched his with a strength he hadn't realized she was capable of. "Despite the fact that you and I don't see eye to eye on everything, I actually like you. I never want to see people I care about hurting."

When he turned to her, tears were freely slipping down her face.

Jack released the tight, hard breath he was holding, allowing the sadness inside him to be released into that one breath. Dust scattered in the air.

"Lucy, there's something you should know." Jack closed his eyes as shame filled him. "It's my fault my brother is dead."

When he opened his eyes, her caring gaze met his.

She wiped her eyes and placed a hand on his arm but said nothing. The warmth of her touch encouraged him to continue.

"We were playing outside. My family lived in Tulsa then. Typical for me, I was so engrossed in reading that I didn't notice when Daniel ran out from in-between two parked cars to chase his ball. Right into the street. He was hit by a car."

A long silence swirled around them.

"How is that your fault?" she whispered.

"I'm the older brother, by minutes. Daniel was…impulsive. It was my job to look after him. That was always understood."

"Oh, Jack, surely you must see what an impossible burden that was for you at that age. Like our friend Dub downstairs. You were a child, Jack. A child. And it was an accident. A tragic accident."

Jack sucked in a breath of air. He wanted to believe that. Desperately. But he couldn't.

"You will never be free until you give this burden to God and let it go."

"I'm sure even God is disappointed in me for that day."

"It's been, what? Over twenty-five years?"

"You don't understand."

"Oh, but I do. I do. There were a thousand what-ifs about that day in the car with my parents."

Jack reached out, and this time it was he who took her hand, enveloping her softness in his large hand as though it was something he did every day. She didn't pull away. "I've never told anyone about this," he murmured.

Lucy nodded.

"My mother left us when Daniel died."

"It's a horrible thing to lose a child. We can never say how we might react." She sighed. "This is why my job at the ranch is so important to me. I want to save all the children." Her voice cracked. "Sometimes you can't, can you?"

"No. I suppose not."

Moments later, he turned his head and met her gaze. "Thank you, Lucy."

"Jack, we're sort of friends now. Friends are there for each other."

"Sort of friends?" The words made him smile.

"Yes," she breathed softly in response.

He still held her hand, and he could feel her pulse jump when she looked at him.

He leaned forward and touched his forehead to hers. "Sort of friends. Right," he said with a soft chuckle. Then he stood and pulled her to her feet. "Come on, let's go down."

"Yes, we better. Your aunt is feeding the children lemonade and cookies. They should be bouncing off the walls by now."

"You left my seventy-eight-year-old aunt with three kids?"

"She was having a great time. Maybe you should consider making promises to Dub more often. She'd love that."

"More promises. That's a little scary."

She patted his arm. "It gets easier every time."

He looked into her eyes and realized that things were only getting easier because of Lucy. That thought alone shook him.

Lucy waved a hand in front Jack's face as he leaned against the pen fence. "Are you awake?"

"I'm sleeping with my eyes open. A trick I learned as a law student riding the subway to class."

"Impressive."

"Not really." He grimaced and shot an accusatory look at the sky. "The sun has risen, so I guess it's too late to go back to bed."

She inhaled and assessed the deep blue panorama overhead. "Don't be silly. This is going to be a lovely day. Not nearly as hot as usual, either."

Jack yawned and stretched. He glanced around. His expressive face clearly said he was unimpressed with the sight of the ranch at 6:00 a.m. "Remind me why you're here?"

"Pardon me?" she squeaked.

"That's not what I meant. I promised Dub. You shouldn't have to be inconvenienced." He pulled out his phone and groaned. "Aren't the horses still sleeping?"

"I'm here because you aren't a certified instructor, thus you are not qualified to take Dub horseback riding alone."

"Did you just insult my equestrian skills?"

"You were on a saddle for the first time since you were a kid two weeks ago. I'm a certified instructor. I'll help you with Dub. My insurance carrier will be much happier that way."

"Fine, boss. So which horses?"

"Dub wants Grace."

"Isn't Grace a bit more horse than a five-year-old can handle?" he asked.

"Grace is a beginner horse. All the kids start on Grace."

He was suddenly wide-awake, his gray eyes round with a pointed accusation. "You put me on a kiddie horse for the trail ride?"

"You did fine."

"That's because I didn't realize I had training wheels."

Lucy laughed. "You hadn't ridden a horse in two decades. What did you expect me to set you loose on?"

"Was everyone laughing behind my back?"

"Not at all. You did great."

"I can't believe Grace never let on. She kept eating those carrots I gave her and never said a word." Jack shook his head with obvious disgust. "So which horse will I be riding today?"

"Chloe. She's spirited, yet very well trained."

"That still doesn't explain why we're doing this so early."

"Apparently your coffee is not doing its job." She slowed her words. "You promised Dub. The stables are very busy during the summer months. There's a sign-up sheet for recreational riding and training. We were completely booked. I had to pull strings to get us this Friday-morning slot."

"Maybe you missed the sign on your parking space, but you're the director," he said.

"That doesn't matter. I play fair."

She assessed his fancy stainless-steel container of coffee. "You know you can't take that on the ride. Right?"

"Why not? I take it in the car."

"When you ride, you focus on the horse, not coffee."

"Yes, Madame Director."

Lucy nodded toward the curb. "Lorna just dropped off Dub."

They both turned in time to see Dub race to the stable entrance in his new riding boots. He wore a red polo shirt tucked neatly into his jeans.

"Wow, Dub, you look like a real equestrian," Lucy said.

"What's that mean?"

"It means you are ready to ride."

He puffed out his chest and looked at Jack. "Ready to go, buddy?"

"I can see you are," Jack said. "Nice boots."

Dub grinned and stared at his feet. "Thanks, Mr. Jack."

Lucy slid open the stable door.

"What's my horse's name again?" Jack asked.

"Chloe."

"Chloe." He started walking down the center aisle of the stable.

"Dub, do you know how to tack a horse?" Lucy asked the little guy.

"Yeth. Leo showed me. 'Cept I'm too little."

"We don't have much time today, so Mr. Jack will tack for you, okay?"

"Okay."

"Tack his horse, Jack?" she called.

Jack nodded as he inspected each stall. When he stopped outside Chloe's stall, his eyes rounded. "Lucy, this horse is as old as your Honda."

"That is not true, and do not let Chloe hear you say that."

He peeked over the stall door. "How about this one instead?"

Lucy carefully chose her words. "Zeus? That gelding is a bit strong-willed."

"I can handle strong-willed." He looked pointedly at her.

"Jack, I really don't think…"

"Lucy, I can handle Zeus."

"Fine. If you insist, but you will wear a helmet."

"I didn't wear one on the trail ride."

"That was with Grace. No helmet, no Zeus. If you keep pushing me, I'll have to insist on a riding vest, as well."

"Helmet it is." He rolled his eyes.

"Role model, Mr. Jack. Role model," she murmured.

Lucy led Grace outside the barn once Jack had the horse saddled up. She gave Dub a boost onto the mare's back. "Collect your reins," she instructed.

"Like this?"

"Very good. Blaze and I are going to walk next to you this session. Grace and Blaze are good friends. Did you know that?"

"They are?"

She nodded.

"Where will we go?" Dub asked.

"Just down the trail to the big corral."

"Keep your hands low and together on her neck," Lucy instructed. She stroked Grace's mane. "You're a good horse, Grace."

Lucy slid her foot in a stirrup and hopped onto Blaze at the same time that Jack trotted past them. Zeus offered an unhappy snort.

"Jack, you're a little tight on the reins. Ease up. Zeus gets cranky if you pull on his mouth."

"I got this."

Zeus began to move faster.

"Don't kick him," Lucy said. "He doesn't like to be kicked. A gentle squeeze will be sufficient."

"Now you tell me!" Jack called back.

The discordant and loud vibrating trill of an old-fashioned alarm clock ripped through the quiet morning.

A cell phone alarm? It must be Jack's.

Clearly distressed, Zeus began to buck.

"Hold on to the horn!" Lucy yelled as Jack flailed back and forth in the saddle.

She turned to Dub. "Keep Grace very still. Okay?"

The little boy nodded.

Lucy clicked her tongue and nudged Blaze toward Jack. "Toss me the phone, Jack."

Without looking, he threw the device in her direction. It bounced on the ground, but the alarm kept going.

Lucy slid off Blaze and scooped up the phone, fiddling with the screen until the noise stopped.

"Whoa. Zeus. Whoa," Jack said. Though he pulled up on the reins, he began to slide sideways off the saddle.

When Zeus finally obeyed and stopped, Jack was dumped unceremoniously to the ground on his backside.

Lucy ran and grabbed the horse's reins.

"Mr. Jack, are you okay?" Dub hollered.

Jack stood, dusted himself off and yanked off his helmet. "Oh, yeah, I'm fine. Cowboys slide off like that to protect the horse. Happens all the time."

Dub stared at him, confusion and concern on his face.

When Dub looked away, Lucy leaned over. "He can't hear you. You can whimper now."

"No, really," Jack said. "I appreciate your concern, Madame Director, but I'm fine. Even though that crazed horse just threw me off, and I could have broken every bone in my body."

She handed him his phone. "You slid to the ground."

"Whatever." Jack stared at the cracked screen and slowly shook his head. Grabbing Zeus's reins from her, he started walking toward the stables.

"Come on, Jack, you have to get back in the saddle. Literally."

"Seriously? This horse hates me."

"I didn't mean Zeus. Chloe would love a morning ride. We'll meet you at the corral."

"Chloe, huh?"

"Yes. You can untack Zeus when we're done. We only have the corral for the next twenty minutes. In the meantime, we're burning daylight."

"You aren't going to say I told you so?"

Lucy put her foot in the stirrup and mounted Blaze. "No. We all make mistakes. The important thing is that we don't waste our time with Dub."

Jack stared at her for moments. Then he nodded. "You're right." A slow smile spread across his face before he turned toward the stable. "Thanks for reminding me of what's important. It's not every day I get to go riding with two of my favorite people."

Lucy's eyes rounded at his words. If he was messing with her, someone needed to notify her heart right away, because it had melted and she was dangerously close to falling for Jack Harris.

# Chapter Ten

"Big Heart Ranch. Lucy Maxwell speaking."

"Maxwell? This is Alberta Hammerton, returning Mr. Harris's call. Is he available?"

"Mr. Harris?" Lucy blinked, confused.

"Yes. Your retreat facility coordinator. I have those quotes he requested."

"May I take your number and have him call you back? He stepped out for a moment."

"Who did you say you are?"

"Lucy Maxwell. Ranch director."

"Thank you, Ms. Maxwell. Oh, and he has my number."

"Perfect."

She dropped the phone into its charger. "Retreat coordinator? Yes. Absolutely perfect."

She turned to her computer, fingers flying across the keyboard until she pulled up the staff and volunteer schedule. A quick search on the spreadsheet directed her to Jack Harris's schedule.

Stall mucking. Knee-deep in horse manure, and the man was still causing problems. A multitasking troublemaker.

The phone rang again, and Lucy grabbed the receiver a second time. "Big Heart Ranch, Lucy Maxwell speaking."

"Oh, I'm terribly sorry to disturb you on a Monday morning, Ms. Maxwell. I know you must be extremely busy. This is Erin with Timber Staffing Agency. May I speak to Mr. Harris?"

"Could I take a message? Mr. Harris is involved in another project at the moment."

"Would you tell him I have two candidates to schedule for interviews?"

"Interviews?"

"Yes. For the admin position. I can assure you that they are both highly qualified. He told me how particular you are."

Lucy took a deep breath. "I'm sure they are. I have your number on caller ID. I'll have him check back with you as soon as he's free."

When the phone rang a third time, she stared at the receiver for a moment, and then began to count backward. "Really, Jack?" she fumed.

"Lucy?" Emma called out. "Is that your phone?"

"Yes. I've got it."

"Maxwell speaking."

"USA Rentals. I've got a sixteen-foot truck available. Do you want to schedule?"

"Truck? What truck?"

"Just a minute." Papers rustled before the man spoke again. "Jack Harris requested a sixteen-foot truck. We've got one ready to go. Does he need furniture pads and a hand cart?"

"I'm not sure. May I have your name and have him call you right back?"

"Roscoe. This is Roscoe. He has my number. I talked to him yesterday. Tell him to hurry before I have to release the truck."

Lucy grabbed the keys to the Ute. "I'll be back," she said when she passed Emma's door.

Parking the Ute outside the stables, Lucy slowly walked through the building, checking stalls on either side of the large space. No Jack Harris in sight, but the stalls were clean—evidence that he'd been by recently.

Tripp was in his office, hunched over a laptop. Lucy gently knocked on the door.

"Come in," he grunted without looking up.

"Ah, Tripp, have you seen our new volunteer, Mr. Harris?"

"Chickens."

"Thanks." She paused. "Everything okay?"

Tripp leaned back in his chair, and his ice-blue eyes pinned her. He absently rubbed the scar that ran down the left side of this face. "Truthfully, Lucy, I could use some help with this paperwork. We talked about hiring someone last spring. It's only getting worse. I'm stuck in here crunching numbers and ordering supplies when I should be out there with the horses and getting ready for the ranch rodeo."

Mouth open in surprise, Lucy simply stared. She'd never heard the taciturn cowboy string together that many sentences at once. "I, um, I'll see what I can do. Right now we're on hold until the budget is approved."

"Don't hang me out to dry."

"I won't forget your request, Tripp."

She carefully closed the door and returned to the Ute, where she sat for several minutes in stunned surprise. Tripp's words and Jack's comments echoed in her ear. Was it possible she was being narrow-minded and inflexible with the ranch budget? Once again, she found herself rethinking her role as director and praying for guidance. "What do You want me to do, Lord?" she whispered.

Lucy buckled her seat belt and headed down the road to the coops. Rue Butterfield met her in the middle of the chicken yard. She held a basket of eggs in one hand and a mangled straw Stetson in the other.

"Rue, what are you up to?" Lucy asked.

"I came by to visit Mrs. Carmody."

"Is there something wrong with our favorite hen?"

"Not at all. We're friends. I like to visit on occasion. We old birds have to stick together."

"Old is not a word I would ever use in connotation with General Rue Butterfield."

"Well, thank you, Lucy."

Lucy glanced around. "Have you seen Jack?"

"Yes. He was here." Rue gestured toward the

basket of eggs. "I offered to wash these and run them over to the chow hall for him."

"Did he mention where he was headed?"

"I believe he said he had to get cleaned up for an appointment in town."

"An appointment." Lucy nodded absently.

"You know, dear, I think there must be something wrong with his schedule."

"What makes you say that?"

"He has stall mucking and chicken coops. Both chores are scheduled every day for the entire summer. We never assign both of those chores together. It's always one or the other."

"It's no mistake. And why not? The man's on a mission to fill Leo's shoes, so I'm helping the process along."

Rue started laughing. "Oh, my," she said, catching her breath as she carefully balanced the eggs. "So he's been doing both all summer? Is that what you're saying?"

She nodded.

"Oh, Lucy, I believe you may have finally met your match."

"My match? What do you mean?"

"Anyone else would have complained about the assignment. Not Jack. He's determined to prove he's not simply a pretty city slicker. The man wants to pull his weight. Or Leo's weight, in this case. You two were cut from the same cloth, if you'll excuse the cliché. Neither of you will back down from a challenge."

"Jack and me? Alike?"

"Yes. You're both single-minded and stubborn."

"Those are my best features, but I'm not so sure that makes me like Jack."

"You might want to give it some thought," Rue said.

"Not likely. I don't sleep at night as it is."

"Lucy, do you mind if I ask what the deal is with Jack?"

"What do you mean?"

"Oh, come on. He's polished, well-educated and reeks of old money. This is a man who probably speaks three languages and went to an Ivy League college. Yet he's running around trying his best to replace Leo and not getting paid for his efforts. I imagine Jack Harris has better things to do with his time than hang out on Big Heart Ranch in the middle of summer, shoveling horse manure."

Lucy was speechless for a moment. Rue had certainly nailed the man. "He's a volunteer," she finally said.

"Yes. I'm aware. And when he's not volunteering?"

"Rue, I'm not sure you really want to know. I don't know if it's a good idea to tell you, either."

"How long have I been working at the ranch, Lucy?"

"Four years."

"Have you ever known me to be indiscreet?"

"No," Lucy murmured.

"The United States government handed me a top secret security clearance. If Uncle Sam trusted me not to sell them out, maybe you could, as well."

"Jack is Meredith Brisbane's nephew. He's the attorney holding up the funding." Lucy released a breath as the words came out in a rush.

Rue's eyes widened with surprise, her mouth sagging open with a gasp. "I never saw that coming." The general began to laugh. "You're telling me that Jack is the jerk who hasn't signed the donation proposal." She laughed again and wiped her eyes. "Oh, the irony."

"Yes, I nearly lost it when he agreed with you on the trail ride."

"You've been protecting him?"

"I suppose I have. I wanted him to evaluate the ranch without bias."

Rue paused and narrowed her eyes. "Are you threatened by Jack Harris, Lucy?"

"I'm intimidated by the fact that he's been here three weeks and has come up with some great ideas for the ranch. Ideas that I, as the director, should have come up with."

"So that's why you're questioning your role at Big Heart Ranch."

"Rue, I've been running everything for five years. Maybe it's time for me to take a back seat. To tell you the truth, as much as I hate to admit it, he's good at what he does. Right now he's screening personal assistant candidates for me."

"Marvelous. You need one."

"Yes. So everyone feels free to tell me."

"Is he going to approve the funding?"

"Most days I'm certain the answer is yes. The rest of the time, he skirts the issue while he explores new ideas for the ranch. We continue to butt heads because he refuses to keep me in the loop."

"Oh, so this is all about control."

"It's my ranch!"

"If he felt like you'd listen to him objectively, he might not be working behind your back."

"Whose side are you on?"

"Are there sides?"

Lucy opened her mouth and closed it.

"Dear, you have to be willing to open that closed fist of yours in order to allow people to help you."

"I'm going to have to think about this," Lucy said. She turned to go and then stopped. "Rue, what's a soiree?"

The general smiled and cocked her head. "I haven't heard that term in a long while. A soiree is like a cocktail party held later in the evening, and usually with some sort of musical entertainment. They're generally quite romantic affairs. I've been to many a soiree in my day," she mused. "Why do you ask?"

"Meredith Brisbane has invited me to a soiree at her estate this weekend."

"Oh, my, isn't that great timing?"

"Why do you say that?"

"Well, she's head of the Brisbane Foundation. She must really like you if she invited you to her soiree. That bodes well for our budget approval."

"I pray you're right." Lucy frowned. "Um, Rue?"

"Yes, dear?"

"What should I wear?"

Rue glanced at Lucy's staff T-shirt, jeans and boots. "Not your red boots."

Lucy sighed. "I was afraid of that."

"A lovely young woman such as yourself certainly has at least one sophisticated dress tucked into the back of her closet."

"Rue, I have flannel shirts tucked into the back of my closet."

"Didn't you have some fancy events while you were in college?"

"I worked at the ranch when I wasn't in class. There was no time for fancy anything."

"You need to get yourself to Tulsa and find a dress and shoes." She assessed Lucy. "A stop at a salon for a trim and manicure are not out of the question, either."

"I don't know the first thing about where to shop in T-town."

"When is this soiree?"

"Saturday."

"Nothing like waiting until the last minute." Rue arched a brow.

"In my defense, it was a last-minute invitation." Lucy glanced down at her daily ranch outfit and sighed. "Who am I kidding? I don't have a clue what I'm doing. My life is spent in jeans and the occasional sundress from the Western store. I have no idea what to wear or the proper etiquette for an event at the foundation."

"Clear your schedule and take Emma with you to the big city."

"Is that really necessary? They have shops in Timber."

"When was the last time you had your hair trimmed?"

"At the start of summer, at the Timber barbershop."

Rue groaned. "Oh, Lucy. The barbershop? Didn't anyone ever tell you that good hair covers a multitude of things?"

"I don't see you with fancy hairdos, General."

"That's by choice. Not omission. There's a difference. I've put in my time in dresses and heels." Rue stopped and looked at Lucy again. "But you. No excuse. You represent the ranch, so you should be prepared to dress for this occasion and others."

"Rue," Lucy groaned.

"You know, Lucy, it's bad enough your childhood was stolen. I will not allow you to go any longer without some girly fun."

"Girly fun?"

"A salon and spa day."

Lucy gulped and stepped back. "I don't do salon and spa days."

"You do now. I'll make all the arrangements for you and your sister. Why, I'll even babysit the twins." She nodded. "I'll inform Emma, so you don't weasel out."

"I don't do salon and spa days," Lucy whined under her breath. She stomped her way to the bunkhouse and pounded on the door. Her hand was raised to knock again when the door swung open and she nearly fell over.

"Whoa," Jack said, catching her fist. "Stand down there, Madame Director."

Freshly showered, his dark hair was combed back and his face cleanly shaven. He looked almost the way he did when she'd first met him. Powerful. In control. The man smelled good, too. For a moment, she simply stared.

"Lucy?"

"I, um…"

"Lucy? Did you need something? I've finished my chores early and I'm not scheduled for the rest of the day." He glanced at his watch.

"Don't let me bother you. Your personal time is your own. I wanted to give you your messages." She held out the pink slips of paper.

Jack winced and pulled out his phone, which was held together by duct tape. "I apologize. This must be really annoying. My phone keeps cutting out. The new one arrives today or tomorrow. I left your number with my contacts."

"Retreat facility coordinator?" she asked. "Really? Was King of the Mountain taken?"

He grimaced. "It's not as bad as it sounds. I have to talk the talk and walk the walk if I want people to take me seriously." He took the papers from her and neatly folded them.

"Take *you* seriously. You. Not me."

"Are you offended that I'm doing this? You did say—"

"I know what I told you, Jack. Yes, in a moment of weakness and complete exhaustion on the trail ride, I agreed that you do can the legwork and present your findings. I simply had no idea you would be moving at the speed of light."

"It only seems like I'm moving fast because you move so slow."

She released a soft gasp. "I can't believe you said that. What's that supposed to mean anyhow?"

"Lucy, it isn't normal to leave a house abandoned for three years. To have a closet full of appliances and household gadgets you never even look at."

"When did I say I was normal?" She gave a sad shake of her head and turned away. "Wow, I never imagined you'd use the confidence I shared with you against me. I trusted you, Jack. I shared my chocolate with you and I trusted you."

"Lucy, wait. I'm sorry. That's not what I meant."

She met his gaze. "What did you mean, Jack?"

"I don't know… I'm just sorry. That was uncalled for."

She paused. "How sorry are you? Sorry enough to sign the proposal?"

He rolled his eyes. "The mission of the foundation is to serve the local community. If I can help the ranch become more self-sufficient, then less money will be needed at Big Heart Ranch, and other organizations will benefit from the Brisbane Foundation funding. So the answer is no. I'm not going to sign anything until my work here is done."

She crossed her arms. "What is this obsession you have with the lodge?"

"It's not an obsession. I'm exploring options."

"Couldn't you explore your options from your office at the estate? You'd even have a phone and an admin."

"I promised my aunt and Dub I'd be at the ranch for the entire summer. I'm sort of locked into Leo's chores, too. You might not miss me, but those chickens would."

Miss him. She hadn't even thought that far ahead. Nor did she want to. It would be far better to simply imagine him gone and pretend he was never here rather than miss him.

"I guess this whole retreat thing is sort of fun for you, isn't it?" she asked.

"Sure. I'll admit I like a challenge."

Lucy nodded, as an odd tightness squeezed her chest. What would happen when he wanted more of a challenge than Lucy and Dub, and Big Heart Ranch in Timber, Oklahoma, could offer? When he left in search of his next adventure?

"You okay, Lucy?"

"I'm fine." She met his gaze. "What's the rental truck for?"

"I'm helping my aunt empty out the stable loft." He glanced at his watch again and straightened his tie. "I really have to go. I'll be back in a couple of hours. We could talk then."

He started down the walk and then stopped. "I finished my chores, if that's what's behind this. In Leo fashion, I might add. Dub and I did arts and crafts this morning."

"I never doubted you for a minute."

He frowned.

"What about the interviews, Jack?"

"I'll handle them until we get down to the final candidates. No use wasting your time until the field is narrowed. I put an ad in the Timber paper, so we still have a few more candidates to review."

"You paid for an ad? To hire an admin I said I can't afford?"

"Utilizing the lodge would eliminate that problem."

"Again with the lodge." She got in the Ute, wishing there was a door she could slam.

"You might be overreacting here, Lucy," he called.

"Who, me? The invisible director of Big Heart Ranch?"

Jack cleared his throat. "This might not be a good time to ask when you want me to shadow you."

"Whenever works with your schedule, Jack. I don't want to inconvenience you."

He nodded, her sarcasm clearly sailing right over his head. "What time?"

"Whenever. Stop by my office. If I'm not there, Emma will know where you can find me."

"Okay."

She nodded. "Jack?"

"Yes?"

"Your tie is crooked."

"Thanks." He glanced down, adjusted the silk material, walked over to the Lexus and got in.

Three weeks at the ranch, and the man remained exactly the same. Aggravatingly perfect and unaffected by his time with them. While she, on the other hand, had been turned upside down. She gave the man an inch and he took far, far more. It was then that Lucy realized with stark clarity that she better start guarding her heart, before he took that, too, because she certainly couldn't handle that sort of disappointment once again.

Jack pulled the Lexus to the curb outside the traditional two-story redbrick house with black shutters. A bicycle lay on the front path. He got out of the car, ready to spend time shadowing Lucy.

He'd give anything to be able to share the news that he'd gotten a great response from the local chamber of commerce regarding the Big Heart Ranch Retreat Center with Lucy. But the ranch director wasn't ready to consider that good news. He'd wait until he had all his cows in a row before he shared everything with her. Maybe then she'd be able to see the big picture.

Down the street, Lucy stood at the back of the Honda pulling grocery sacks from the trunk. He picked up speed and met her on the sidewalk outside the house. She glanced through him.

"Let me help you," Jack said.

"I don't need help," she returned, rushing toward the house steps ahead of him.

"Are you mad at me?"

"Mad? No. I'm aggravated, irritated and annoyed."

"Fair enough. Where are you going in such a hurry?"

"I have sick house parents. They have the flu, as do two of the kids in the house."

"What can you do about that?"

"I'm going to take over for them. Cook, clean and handle the kids until they feel better."

"I'll help."

"You signed up to shadow me at the office." She stopped and turned around, assessing his khaki slacks and polo shirt. "I don't think you're up for this particular assignment."

"I can handle anything you can, Madame Director."

"Have you had your flu shot, Jack?"

"All up-to-date."

"Okay, but don't say I didn't warn you." Lucy offered an ominous chuckle and kept walking up to the front door, where Dub stood at the screen.

"Dub," Jack said. "What are you doing here?"

The little boy laughed. "I live here, Mr. Jack." He looked to Lucy. "Mr. Bill and Miss Lorna are resting. They have a fever and sick stomachs."

Lucy pulled open the screen. "Where's your big brother?"

"He's upstairs getting ready for work."

"Work?" Jack asked. He followed her into the neat two-story home.

"Yes. Many of our high school students have jobs in the community during the summer."

"Dub, whose bicycle is that on the sidewalk?" Jack asked as he stepped into the home.

"Stewie's. Mine is in the garage. I take real good care of the bicycle you gave me, Mr. Jack."

Jack grinned, foolishly pleased that Dub was riding his old bike.

"Where are Stewie and Henry?" Lucy asked.

"In bed. They're sicker. They puked even."

Jack grimaced, and his stomach clenched. "So that's the ripe odor around here."

Rue Butterfield came down the carpeted stairway with her medical bag in her hand. "Lucy. Jack. I see the cavalry has arrived."

"I'm not so sure about that. How is everyone?" Lucy asked.

"Quite the flu epidemic we have going on at the boys' ranch."

"Don't tell me that. You offered the flu vaccine last spring. Didn't anyone take you up on that?"

Rue raised a hand in gesture. "The joys of modern medicine. Apparently, another strain has hit the ranch. The good news is that this seems to be a hard-hitting and short-lasting virus."

"Good news, huh?" Lucy returned. "I'm out of replacement house parents."

"We've isolated our patients. Hopefully, things will slow down. Remind everyone of the importance of good hand washing. Are you aware that the flu virus lasts up to twenty-four hours on hard surfaces?"

"Ugh, I had no idea." Lucy walked over to the counter and pulled two containers of antiseptic wipes from a grocery sack. "However, I did bring these."

"Excellent. Wipe down anything that isn't moving."

Dub's eyes rounded and he hid behind Jack. "Not me!"

"No." Rue laughed. "Not you."

"Thanks, Rue." Lucy sighed. "This has been some summer, hasn't it?"

"I like staying busy," Rue replied. "Retirement is for old people. This is much more fun."

"Still, this has been ridiculous and over-the-top busy."

"True." Rue washed her hands and addressed Jack. "And look at you. You're quite the volunteer. Trail rides, stall mucking, chicken coops and now house parent duty?"

"Jack-of-all-trades. Pun intended," he said.

Behind him, Lucy scoffed.

Rue eyed Jack as she rolled down her sleeves. "What is it you do when you're back in your world?" She winked at Lucy.

"I'm sort of between worlds right now."

"Between worlds. I like that, and how fortunate for us."

"Not everyone agrees." He met Lucy's gaze.

"Oh, I don't know," Rue said. "I can provide you with a list of folks around here who are very thankful you've been with us this summer. We couldn't have done it without you, Jack. Especially with those budget issues hanging over our heads, stressing everyone out."

Again, Lucy met his gaze and the arrow of guilt pierced his conscience. Time to step up the work on the lodge.

A small hand tugged at his shirt tail. "Mr. Jack. Can we have lunch now?"

"Sure." He smiled. "Will you excuse us, General?"

"Absolutely. I need to head home to clean up and have lunch myself." She saluted them on her way out the door. "I'm sure I'll see you two soon."

"Thanks for stopping in," Lucy called.

"We gots pizza in the freezer," Dub said.

"How does soup and sandwiches sound instead?" Lucy dug into the grocery sacks she'd brought with her.

"Pizza sounds really good," Dub repeated.

"I agree," Jack said. "Frozen pizza is in my limited repertoire, too."

"Does that mean we can have pizza?" Dub asked.

"It sure does." Jack opened the freezer and assessed the box. "How many should I take out?"

"One should do the trick. There's just the three of us," Lucy said. She leaned over to read the instructions on the back and then turned on the oven.

"Don't forget the baby," Dub said.

"Baby?" Jack looked down at Dub. "There's a baby here who eats pizza?"

Dub giggled. "She doesn't eat pizza."

"The baby is sleeping," Lucy said.

"Wanna see the baby?" Dub asked him.

"Not particularly," Jack admitted.

"The pizza will take twenty minutes," Lucy said. "Maybe you can look in on the kids while you're waiting. I'll start loading the dishwasher."

"You mean the *sick* kids?" he asked.

"Yes. Stewie and Henry. The baby isn't sick."

"But you want me to check the baby, as well?"

"Yes," Lucy said.

"What am I checking the baby for?"

"If she's awake, check her diaper."

"Check it for what? Its existence?"

"Very funny." She frowned at him. "Check and see if it needs to be changed."

He raised a palm. "Nope. Stop right there. I don't change diapers."

"Jack, in a perfect world, no one would change diapers."

"Lucy, I'm willing to do a lot of things outside my comfort zone, and I think I've proven that over the last month, but changing diapers is not one of them."

"Someone has to do it, and you asked to shadow me today. In fact, you insisted."

He groaned and ran a hand through his hair. "Have you really thought this through? Sending me in there is not in the baby's best interest."

"Seriously, Jack? Are you making this up?" She stared at him, exasperation raw on her face.

"I wouldn't know how to make this up," he said with a grimace.

She dried her hands and faced him again. "Are you able to take out trash? Or is that outside your comfort zone?"

"Trash?" He perked up. "Yes. Trash happens to be my specialty. I'll handle all the trash."

"Terrific. When you're done I'll give you some chores from the children's chart."

Jack assessed the chore chart with its little gold stars for a job well-done. "This day isn't turning out quite the way I'd anticipated," he muttered.

"Tell me about it."

He grabbed the trash and headed outside. When he returned, Dub was waiting at the door.

"Mr. Jack? I don't feel so good." Dub rubbed a hand over his stomach.

What? Wait. No. This could not be happening. Jack whipped around. Where was Lucy? He picked up the baby monitor and yelled into the device. "Lucy!"

She raced downstairs, her feet thundering on the steps, eyes frantic with concern. "What is it? Why did you do that? You woke up the baby."

"Dub doesn't feel good."

She sighed and laid a hand on Dub's forehead. "Get him into bed. I'll be up to take his temperature."

"What are you going to do?" Jack asked.

"I'm calling Emma to come and take the baby." Lucy handed Jack a plastic bucket.

He met her gaze and shook his head. "Is this for what I think it's for?"

"Yes. Take it, Jack, you may need it."

"I don't want to need it."

Lucy jammed her hands on her hips. "Jack, get him up those stairs right now."

"Yes, ma'am." He grabbed the bucket, scooped up Dub and took the stairs two at a time. "Which room is yours?"

Dub pointed to the first door. Jack peeked in. Stewie and Henry were asleep in bunk beds.

"Are you going to be sick?" he whispered.

"No, but my head hurts. Can you pray for me?"

"I, ah…"

"Please Mr. Jack?"

"Sure, Dub. Get under the covers." Jack pulled back the sheet and the blanket on the twin bed and handed Dub a stuffed turtle from under the pillow. When Dub was settled, Jack held his small hand. "Lord, please help my buddy Dub feel better, and everyone in this house. Amen."

"Amen. Thanks, Mr. Jack." Dub's lower lip quivered. "I don't like being sick."

"It's going to be okay. Close your eyes."

"Will you sit with me until I fall asleep?"

"Absolutely, buddy."

Dub's eyes fluttered closed, and Jack gently pushed the flyaway blond hair from his forehead. His little face was flushed, particularly high on his cheeks, with the emerging illness. Within minutes the regular rise and fall of the five-year-old's chest said he was asleep.

Jack was hesitant to leave. Finally, he tucked

the covers carefully around Dub and eased off the edge of the bed.

"Oh, Dub," he whispered. "How did you manage to crawl right inside my heart when I wasn't looking?"

Jack's steps were slow as he left the room.

Lucy met him at the bottom of the stairs. "How's he doing?"

"Asleep." He headed to the sink to wash his hands.

"Good job, Jack. Gold stars for you."

"Yeah. Even though I'm diaper-phobic?"

"We all have our proficiencies. And deficiencies. Did he...you know?"

"Nope. I'm beyond grateful."

The oven pinged, and Lucy turned off the alarm and slid the pizza out. "Lunch."

"I'm not hungry anymore." He leaned against the counter. "So what do we do now? What's Plan B?"

"Jack, this *is* Plan B."

"Yeah? How do parents do this? I've only been here a short time, yet I can tell you this was harder than Mrs. Carmody and mucking out stalls combined."

Lucy smiled. "I know, but when you love someone you do anything for them. There's a lot of love around these homes."

"Even though they aren't their biological kids?"

"That's not even a consideration, Jack. Falling

in love with a child has nothing to do with biology. It's a choice." She wiped the counter down with an antiseptic wipe. "There's something to love about every child."

"I'm not sure I could do what they do."

"You did it today."

He paused at her words. "I did what I had to. For Dub."

"That's the start of parenting. Common sense, love and putting their needs before your own." She shrugged. "Nobody looks forward to cleaning up after a sick child. It's part of the job description, offset by the moments when they look up at you like you're Superman."

"Superman?"

"That's the way Dub looks at you."

"He does?"

"You've never noticed?"

"Maybe I've tried not to notice. Summer is more than half over. Not a day goes by that I don't think about what will happen to Dub at the end of summer." He looked at her. "Have you thought any more about fostering?"

"Yes, but I'm not sure I'm suitable. My job is pretty demanding. I don't know that I'm a good candidate."

"You raised your siblings, right? If you don't want to raise another family, that's understandable."

"No, that's not what I'm saying. I suppose that

after my engagement debacle, I stopped thinking about my own family. I blocked out the idea. It was safer that way. Now I'm really doubting myself."

"Lucy, I can't think of anyone who would be a better candidate than you. Look how you handled tonight."

"You helped, Jack."

He laughed. "I took out the trash."

She shrugged, obviously dismissing the topic. "What are you going to do when the summer is over?"

"Who knows? I did sublet my place in the city."

"Not going back to New York?" Her eyes widened.

He met her gaze, his own skimming over her brown eyes, her pert nose. "Oklahoma is growing on me."

Lucy shook her head. "Your lips were moving, but the words were all wrong. It sounded like you said Oklahoma is growing on you."

Jack laughed. "Funny."

"Look, Jack, um, I need to apologize. I overreacted yesterday. I promised you could gather information for your project and present it to me, and I intend to keep that promise."

"I appreciate that, and you'll be glad to know I'm almost done."

"Are you?"

"Yeah." He nodded toward the laptop she had

set up on the kitchen table. "Looks like you're working on a project, as well. What's all this?"

"We've got another big milestone event at the ranch coming up a week from Saturday. The annual alumni barbecue and rodeo."

"Tripp's been grumbling about it at the bunkhouse. Big deal, according to him."

"It is a big deal," she said. "It's the end of summer for the kids visiting from the Pawhuska orphanage, and at the same time, all the children who graduated and left the ranch return. It signifies the official end of summer is upon us. Another year is about to begin."

"Sounds like fun."

"Really? I was sure you'd balk."

"I like hot dogs and hamburgers as much as the next guy, Lucy."

"You and Dub will need to sign up for a few events, as well."

"Events?"

"The usual. Three-legged race, tug-of-war, that sort of thing."

"What about you?"

"Stewie and Henry are my buddies. We'll be out there."

"Can't wait for more of that healthy competition."

Lucy glanced at the wall clock. "Things have settled down here. You can go ahead and go. The worst is over. I've got work to do, so I'll spend the night on the couch monitoring the situation. No doubt Lorna and her husband will be able to take over in the morning."

"Are you sure?"

"I am. And Jack?"

"Yeah?"

"About Saturday."

"You aren't begging off, are you? My aunt is looking forward to your presence at her soiree."

"No. I'll be there. In fact, I'll meet you there."

"Lucy, I'm happy to drive you."

"There's no need. We're both attending, but it's not like it's a date or anything."

"Right. We wouldn't want to take a chance on this looking like a date." He glanced around. "Have you seen my keys?"

Lucy lifted up a stack of papers on the counter.

"Ah, there they are." Jack reached around her and scooped up the keys at the same moment she turned right into him.

Jack froze, waiting, watching. His heart kicked up its rhythm a notch as Lucy Maxwell stood very still in the circle of his arms.

Her gaze dropped to his lips, mere inches away, and then moved to his eyes. "I…" She opened her mouth and closed it very slowly. "Thank you again for your help."

Her soft breath touched his face like a caress.

Jack longed to lower his lips to hers. Instead,

he nodded and stepped away with more regret than he would have imagined when he landed at Big Heart Ranch.

"In and out and no one gets hurt," Lucy murmured. "Ask open-ended questions. Gather information, but share little." She stood in the Brisbane estate foyer, handing the silver threaded silk pashmina that Rue had gifted her to a maid before pausing to review Rue's soiree mingle advice one last time.

"Lucy? Is that you?"

She frowned and turned at Jack's voice.

"You know, I thought you ate, slept and lived horses and kids. Who knew there was a different Lucy outside Big Heart Ranch?"

"What are you talking about? I don't look any different." A glance at herself in the hall mirror confirmed her words.

Jack did a slow and appreciative assessment, from her satin heels to her demure black dress. He swallowed. "Oh, yeah, you do. Lucy, you're more lovely than you can possibly imagine."

"That's silly. It's only a dress." Lucy stole another peek at herself, noting the pink that warmed her face. She wasn't accustomed to such flattery, but she could easily get used to Jack's sweet words.

"It's not just the dress. That little frown line across your forehead is gone, and you're relaxed."

She laughed. "Hot stone massage. Every muscle in my body is happy."

"Really?"

"Yes. Followed by a mud bath. Emma and I had a salon and spa day, courtesy of the general."

"That's great. You deserve that and more. You work far too much." Jack cocked his head and looked at her again. "Your hair…" He gestured with a wave of his hand. "Something's different there, too."

"Oh, that. I brushed it."

He laughed. "You're in good spirits, as well."

Her own gaze swept over his charcoal blazer, striped dress shirt—open at the neck—and white slacks. "What about you? You look all cricket and polo and lawn parties, Mr. Harris."

Jack offered a half smile that nudged a dimple to life. The effect was potent, forcing her to glance away as she recalled the almost kiss earlier in the week that had left her weak-kneed and confused.

"Is that a good thing?" he asked.

"It is. You know, Jack, something about you has changed since I met you at that budget meeting at the start of summer."

"Changed?"

"Yes. You smile more."

"I have more to smile about than I did then."

He left her to ponder his words as he took her arm and led her away.

"Let me show you around my aunt's house. Have you ever seen the great room?"

"No. I've never seen anything except the boardroom and the solarium."

"My apologies. We have been remiss."

Jack opened the double doors of the great room and flipped on a switch. The reflective lights of an unusual crystal chandelier lit up the room.

The walls were buttercream, the carpet Aubusson in ribbon patterns of pale blue. Robin's-egg-blue satin couches faced each other around a circular glass coffee table with a crystal bowl of potpourri in the center. The faint scent of lemongrass and verbena welcomed them.

"That chandelier is amazing," Lucy said.

"A wedding present from my uncle. All imported Belgian crystal. If you look closely, you can see that many of the crystal pendalogues are heart-shaped."

"That's so romantic."

"Would that be the way to your heart, Lucy?"

She laughed. "Not exactly. Where would I put a crystal chandelier? And who would clean the crystals?"

"Ever practical."

"How did they meet?" Lucy asked.

"My uncle's family is Native American, and they've owned this land since before statehood. He was a bachelor for a long time. Apparently he'd given up on the idea of marrying."

Lucy nodded thoughtfully as her gaze went to the portraits that filled an entire wall.

"When they found oil on the land, Aunt Meri was with the team of assessors from the oil company."

"Your aunt worked for the oil company? In what capacity?"

"She's a geologist."

"I never knew that."

"As my aunt tells the story, it was love at first sight, for both of them. If you can believe that."

"I'm not sure I do."

"Right. That wouldn't fit into your Plan B theory, would it?"

When he said it like that, she realized that she did sound like a pessimist. But love at first sight? Could that possibly be real?

Jack met her gaze and offered a rueful smile before he continued. "She quit her job when they got married. Uncle Jeb was much older than her and they didn't want to waste any time."

"No children?"

"None."

"So your father is her brother?"

"That's correct."

"Who is this?" Lucy asked, pointing to the picture of twins on the wall.

His voice softened. "That's me and my brother, Daniel."

"You're a twin." She looked at Jack's profile

and then back to the picture several times. "An identical twin. You never told me. You only said that you were older."

He shrugged. "I was. By minutes."

"Do you have other siblings?"

"No. Daniel was my one shot, and I blew it."

Lucy inhaled sharply at his words. "You're so hard on yourself. Doesn't everyone deserve a second chance? That's what Big Heart Ranch is all about," she said softly.

"Yeah, I get that, but don't we need to pay for the mistakes of yesterday?"

"Yesterday is long gone, Jack. Stop bringing it back. His blessings are new every morning. I think it's time for you to start looking ahead and not behind."

He paused as though considering her words, and glanced at the picture one last time. "I'm spoiling the party. Come on, let's go find some of those expensive hors d'oeuvres my aunt is serving."

Lucy was only too aware of his hand on her back as Jack led her through the open doors of a large room. Her gaze spanned the high walls of the room that reached up to a domed vaulted ceiling and back down to the marble floors.

"This is even bigger than the great room."

"Aptly called a ballroom."

"I thought soirees were a bit more intimate of an affair."

"This is intimate to Meredith Brisbane." He

glanced toward the buffet table. "Uh-oh, she's headed this way. Once Aunt Meri corners you, you'll be stuck chatting with a dozen people you don't know."

"Rue prepped me."

He laughed. "I've been doing this all my life. No one can prep you for my aunt's people."

At the far end of the room, the music began. A small trio provided slow jazz sounds. Though the room was large, the music and dim lighting created intimacy.

"Providence is in your court," Jack murmured. "My aunt's been sidetracked and has accepted an invitation to dance from a silver-haired gentleman."

"Good for her," Lucy said.

"What about you, Lucy?" Jack asked. "Would you care to dance?"

She hesitated as he held out a hand.

"One dance." He repeated the request, his dark eyes intent.

"Yes." The word slipped from her mouth while her heart whispered that this was a very bad idea.

Jack caught her by the waist and hummed as he led her across the dance floor.

"I've never glided before," Lucy murmured. "In fact, I'm not much of a dancer."

"Sure you are. It's a partnership, and you've got the right partner. Stick with me. We might even do a little foxtrot later."

"You're very good," she said. They turned and swayed, and he led her past Meredith and her dance partner.

"My aunt is pretty much responsible for every good thing there is about me."

"Dance lessons?"

He nodded and dipped her slightly, his face close enough to smell the faint sandalwood tones of his aftershave.

As the music came to a close, he directed her to the open French doors that led to a veranda. "Wait right here and I'll go in search of sustenance."

Lucy stepped outside, rested her arms on the marble rail and looked out into the garden below. Strings of twinkling white lights had been wrapped around the trees and glittered festively in the night. Overhead a full moon had made an appearance for the event. It rode high in the sky, a hazy blue disc against a carpet of black velvet spilling a generous amount of light onto the world below. The sweet scent of freesias filled the air, and she inhaled deeply.

Lucy sighed at the perfection of the evening. Had she ever imagined an evening with Jack Harris's arms around her on the dance floor? An evening pretending she wasn't a foster child who ran a ranch for kids? Maybe for a few moments she could imagine she was simply a woman enjoying the company of an attentive man.

She glanced at her fingers splayed on the marble

rail. She'd gotten a manicure at the spa. This was the first time in a long time that her nails weren't torn and ragged, and her hands weren't reddened and chapped from the daily ranch chores.

Tonight she was Cinderella at the ball.

And yet it couldn't last. This was Jack's world. Not hers.

Jack returned a moment later, balancing a plate full of food in one hand and two glasses of sparkling water in the other.

"Why do I think you've done this before?" she said.

He winked. "I'm an expert. Check my jacket pocket for silverware and napkins."

Lucy laughed as she pulled the utensils from his blazer.

"Won't your aunt be looking for us?"

"No worries, the night is young. There's still plenty of time for boring conversation with my aunt's acquaintances."

"Acquaintances? Not friends?"

"Money only buys acquaintances and ex-fiancées."

"I see your mantra is intact, as well."

His lips curved into a small smile of acknowledgment.

Lucy speared a bit of food onto her fork and inspected it for a moment. "What is this?"

"That looks like foie gras."

"Which is…?"

"Ah, some things are best to enjoy. I'll explain later." He took a long drink of water. "By the way, I've been sharing business cards for the Big Heart Ranch Retreat Center with a few very select guests."

She stiffened. "What business cards?"

Jack swallowed and held up a hand. "That was a misstep. We aren't talking business tonight." He reached out and touched her forehead with his finger. "Relax that frown."

"Jack, you're pitching a venue that hasn't even been approved. And even if it is, there are still licenses and business plans to complete. I thought we had a deal here."

"We do. Calm down."

"Calm down?"

Her eyes widened with uncertain surprise as Jack leaned forward until his lips touched hers. Her head began to spin and her heartbeat raced, but she kissed him back, without hesitation. When he raised his lips from hers, Lucy kept her eyes closed for a moment. A moment to block out the real world where men like Jack Harris didn't kiss women like her. For tonight she could pretend.

*"What was that?"* Lucy murmured when they broke apart, a hand to her mouth.

"I was trying to change the subject before everything went south. Did it work?"

She blinked. "I…um…"

"Are you all right?" Jack murmured.

"I'm not sure," she whispered, meeting his concerned gaze.

"Should I apologize?"

"Can I get back to you on that?"

"Sure." He ran a hand over his face. "Am I forgiven for bringing up business?"

"Jack?"

"Yeah?"

"My head is spinning. I'm going to need you to talk a little less." She took a deep breath and quickly stepped away from the veranda railing. "We should return to the party. Right away, before I forget I'm only visiting your world."

# *Chapter Eleven*

"Ready to ride, little buddy?"

Dub leaned against the door of the stables with his helmet in his hand and looked around. "Are we going without Miss Lucy?"

"She'll be along." At least he hoped she would be. This was Monday, and she'd had all of Sunday to think about that kiss. As far as first kisses went, it was a good kiss. A simple kiss, yet a good start. Surely Lucy had come to that same conclusion.

Jack glanced around the stable. No Lucy.

*Maybe not.*

What was he thinking, kissing the director of Big Heart Ranch? He was a professional here with a job to do. It didn't include kissing.

"Why don't we tack up our horses while we wait for Miss Lucy?" he asked Dub.

"I'm too little. I can't reach Grace."

"You can help me with Grace. You tell me what to do and I'll do it. Deal?"

Dub's laughter trilled into the morning air.

Jack smiled. He was going to miss that laugh.

"So what's first?"

"Brush Grace so there's nothing under the saddle that could scratch her." Dub handed Jack the brush. "Then you gots to rub her behind the ears and tell her she's a very good horse. She likes that." His face was solemn as he observed Jack's actions.

Grace snorted and snuffled with pleasure at the rub down. "How did I do?"

"Pretty good, Mr. Jack. You're lots better than when you first got here. You're as good as Leo now."

"Whoa, Dub. I appreciate that, buddy."

"Put on the pad. Miss Lucy says to put it a little bit over the withers.

Jack grabbed the flannel pad and positioned it on Grace. It landed slightly crooked, and Dub jumped up to straighten the edges.

"Dub, have you grown?"

"Yeth, Miss Lorna says I'm growing out of my clothes." He grinned with pride.

Jack stared into space for a minute. Dub was growing. Summer was almost over. Soon the little guy would outgrow his riding boots. Who would get him new ones? Who would take Dub riding? Would his new foster home even care that Dub loved Grace?

"Mr. Jack, are we going to the rodeo on Saturday?"

"Sure are."

"Stewie and Henry say they're going to win the greasy pig."

"Greased pig?"

Dub nodded.

Jack sighed. "You really want to try to wrestle a pig, huh?"

"Yeth, please."

Jack grabbed the saddle and hoisted it carefully onto Grace. "So chasing a greasy pig is supposed to be fun?"

"Uh-huh."

He narrowed his eyes and tried to imagine the pig scenario. "Nope. I don't see it, but I respect your right to try. I'll sign you up."

"You'll come watch, too?"

"Of course. We're buddies. Amigos. Pals. We support each other."

"And the sheep?"

"The sheep what?"

"Mutton busting, Jack," Lucy said from behind him. "My team won last year."

"A nice girl like you busts mutton?" He secured the saddle into position and lowered the cinches and stirrups before turning to Lucy.

She laughed. "No. The little kids…"

When his gaze landed on her lips, Lucy paused, suddenly flustered, her face pink. She quickly turned to Dub. "You ride the sheep, right, Dub? Tell him about it."

"We ride without a saddle," Dub explained.

"Isn't that cruel?" Jack asked.

"Bareback. I know some rodeos use a saddle, but we do not. In fact, we're quite humanitarian about it. Even the greased pig competition is one-on-one. We don't let our pigs or sheep get trampled by kids."

"A humanitarian rodeo. Good to know. I'm down with the pig, but the whole bareback mutton thing seems a little harsh."

"Maybe you could observe first, before you make any snap sheep judgments."

"I'll try to be objective, but no promises." He tightened the cinches, checking the tightness before he looked up at Lucy. "What's today's plan for our riding lesson?"

"I checked the stable records. You've gotten in over ten hours with a certified instructor—me. I'm going to authorize you to ride the corral with Dub on your own."

"Whoa. I graduated?"

"Yes. You did."

He lifted his hand for a high-five with Dub.

"Way to go, Mr. Jack."

"Couldn't have done it without you, pal."

"Continue to ride Chloe and keep Dub on Grace. Everyone wears a helmet, and you stay in the corral. No new maneuvers, please."

"No worries. I can't afford another cell phone." Lucy chuckled.

"So you're leaving?" he asked.

"I am. I have a ton of work and two buddies of

my own to fit into my day." She paused. "By the way, I found out what foie gras is."

"Delicious, right?" He grinned.

"Not the word I was looking for. Let's just say that it was wise of you not to tell me at the party."

Jack leaned closer. "Are we okay, Lucy?"

"Okay?"

He shrugged. "You know."

"Oh, that. We're fine," she said, quickly dismissing the subject.

"Hey, did I mention your admin starts next Monday?"

"Oh, which one did you hire?"

"Iris. You said her résumé put her up front."

"Yes. But that doesn't mean you're going to take my input. You've been here over four weeks and have pretty much ignored every single one of my recommendations, unless push comes to shove or a cell phone is destroyed."

"That's not true."

"It's absolutely true. Case in point—the lodge. Guest ranch, rec center, vacation rental." She waved a hand in the air. "Whatever you're calling the place these days."

"Big Heart Ranch Retreat Center."

Lucy crossed her arms. "I'm getting impatient. When will you have your presentation ready?"

"Soon, really soon."

"I hope so. It's been a month."

"Wednesday is a month. It takes time for due diligence."

"It took you five minutes to decide I was a crook."

"I was wrong. Which is why I want to be more thorough."

"You're running out of time for thoroughness. If I don't have a signed proposal or a check in hand soon, we can close the gates and send everyone home."

"Summer is over in two weeks, Lucy. I get that."

"What about the gala?" she continued.

"That's Aunt Meri's thing. My aunt loves a party. If anything stands in the way of that gala, she'll pretty much shoot me. The Brisbane Foundation will cover the expenses for the gala in full."

Lucy released a breath. "Thank you."

Jack looked over his shoulder at Dub, who was happy to walk Grace around the yard outside the stables in circles. "What will happen to Dub?"

"You keep asking me, but you know these things take time." She sighed and clasped her hands together. "I'm working on that, Jack. In fact, I need to get back to my office to work on a stack of paperwork."

"Paperwork? Why not wait until Iris starts and let her help you with your paperwork?"

"This is time-sensitive. I'm applying to the

State of Oklahoma Department of Human Services for their Bridge Foster Program."

"You're really doing it?" A joy he hadn't felt in a long time welled up inside at her words. Jack grabbed Lucy around the waist and swung her around.

"Jack, stop. Put me down."

"Lucy, this is fantastic."

"Please. Keep this confidential. If it doesn't work out, I don't want to disappoint them. The end-of-summer transition from Big Heart Ranch is going to be difficult enough. If they get excited about this and it falls through, they'll be devastated." Lucy sighed. "I'll be devastated. Besides, you know how I feel about promises."

He stared at her, speechless for a few moments at her admission. "You've really applied to foster Dub, Ann and Eva?"

She nodded.

"Lucy, you are amazing."

"Don't give me too much credit. And please don't tell anyone. I may not be approved."

"Don't be ridiculous, Lucy. Everyone approves of you."

"Jack, I'm serious. I don't want anyone to find out. You know, just in case."

"Right. In case the other boot falls. In case the zombies take over. Especially in case Plan B doesn't work, either."

Her expression faltered for a brief moment at his words.

"Oh, Lucy." Unable to resist, Jack snaked his arm around her waist and gave her a swift kiss.

Lucy put a hand to her mouth and stared at him, her face flushed with color. "Jack!" She backed up and looked around. "What are you thinking?"

"That you are a generous and giving woman."

"Thank you, but you can't kiss me in public."

As quickly as the kiss of a moment ago was over, a thought raced through his mind and he froze, stunned. Dub wasn't the only one he was going to miss. He'd miss Lucy Maxwell as much as the little guy.

How had that happened?

Jack turned to Travis. "What's this?"

"What?" The cowboy stopped cleaning his boots to glance over at Jack.

"There's a box on my bed."

"Yeah. It was there when I got here. Looks like a hatbox to me."

Jack opened the round box and unfolded the tissue inside. "What is this?"

"Jack, I know you're a city boy, but I'm thinking even you greenhorns know a straw Resistol when you see one."

"Resistol?"

"Yeah, see that Resistol insignia pin on the band?" Travis shook his head. "That's not a cheap hat, either. The ranch will be full of lovely ladies today. Wear it with pride, bro."

Jack put the hat on his head, examined himself in the mirror and laughed.

"Good fit," Travis said. "Someone knows your hat size."

"Yeah, and they got it big enough to fit my ego. Only one person could have done that."

"My sister, huh?"

"Exactly." He looked at himself again. "You don't think I look a little ridiculous?"

"Jack, a man never looks ridiculous in a hat if he earns the right to wear it. You've put in the time this summer. You earned the right."

"Thanks," Jack murmured.

Travis looked him up and down. "Going to the rodeo, right?"

"Yeah, me and Dub."

"You need a proper shirt. Thankfully, you've come to the right place. I've got shirts." Travis opened his closet and fingered through over two dozen crisply starched and ironed Western shirts. "This one." He handed Jack a black-and-blue plaid Western shirt with snap buttons and black pipe trim on the pockets.

Jack grinned. "Thanks, Travis."

"I'll expect it returned in the same condition."

"Absolutely."

Tripp stepped into the bunkhouse and stood for a minute, staring at Jack without saying anything. Then he went to his drawer and pulled out a belt and brass buckle and handed them to him.

"Here."

Jack's eyes widened at the oversized trophy buckle with a cowboy and bronc engraved on the front, along with the words Guthrie Frontier Days. "Thanks, Tripp."

Tripp nodded and left the bunkhouse without another word.

Jack put the shirt on over his T-shirt and then pulled the belt through the loops on his jeans. He adjusted the hat on his head. "You're sure I should wear this hat?"

"I'm not telling you again," Travis said. "Cowboys wear hats. It keeps your head cool, keeps the sun off your face and keeps the dirt out of your eyes. A cowboy without a hat just ain't right."

"Is that a song?"

"Could very well be."

Jack nodded and pushed his hat to the back of his head and scooped up his keys. "Thanks again, Travis."

"No problem."

Jack strode back across the rodeo grounds for twenty minutes, past cowboys and cowgirls of all ages and sizes before finally admitting to himself he was lost. The ranch was packed with people, but so far the only thing that called his name was barbecued chicken and beef. If he didn't find someone familiar soon, he was going to give up and go eat.

The tent in front of him displayed a colorful banner announcing musical performances on the hour. He stuck his head inside and looked up and down the bleachers.

"Jack?"

He turned to see Rue in a white fringed Western shirt and denim skirt with boots. When he realized her straw hat was exactly like his own, he stood a little straighter.

"Look at you," she said with a sly grin. "Our temporary cowboy looks like one of the locals today."

"You don't think it's too much?"

"Too much what?" She smiled. "Take a peek around you, cowboy. You blend right in with this crowd."

"That's a relief."

"Are you here for the yodeling competition?"

"What?" He stepped back out of the tent. "No. I'm looking for Dub. Do you know where the children's competition is being held?"

"Right over there."

She pointed left, and he took off. A moment later, a small hand slipped into his. "Jack, I like your hat. It matches mine."

He glanced down at the little boy. "So it does."

"Miss Lucy got it for me. She got one for Ann

and Eva, too. They have pink hats." He laughed. "I didn't know cowboys could have pink hats."

Jack pulled out his phone and checked the time. "We've got to hurry and find the greased pig competition."

Dub grabbed his arm. "We're right there. It's in that corral."

"Did you tell Miss Lorna you'd be with me?"

"Yeth."

"Are you sure you want to do this?"

"I've been practicing."

"How do you practice?"

"I chase Stewie and Henry."

Jack laughed. "But listen, Dub, I've been studying up on this, as well."

"You've been studying greased pig?"

Jack looked up. Lucy smiled at him, nearly knocking him off his feet. She wore the yellow sundress with her red boots. The one that made her look like a sunflower. The one she'd been wearing when they met.

"Wow, you're the whole package today, aren't you?" she said, assessing his clothes. "Even have a Western shirt and buckle."

"Courtesy of my roommates." He nodded toward her hat. "I see we all match."

"I thought it might be easier to find you and Dub, but everyone pulled out their straw hats today."

"Thank you for the Resistol," Jack said.

"Yeth! Thank you, Miss Lucy."

"You're both welcome. Now tell me about this greased pig strategy."

"No way. You're the competition," he said.

Lucy sighed, feigning disappointment. "Are you going to be that way?"

"I am, and Dub is going to win today."

Dub grinned when Jack led him to a private area.

"Show me your left hand," Jack said.

Dub shot up his left hand.

"The pig is going to go left, so you have to be ready. Always be prepared to go left. Grab him around the neck, land on his back and hook him with your feet so he can't go anywhere."

Dub offered a solemn nod as he took in the instructions. "How do you know the pig will go left, Mr. Jack?"

"Google." Jack patted his back. "Do your best. That's all you can do."

The announcer called out Dub's name and Jack stood at the fence, hands gripping the rail.

That was his kid in there.

The crowd roared when the gate opened, releasing a sow covered in grease. Dub's little legs moved down the field after the squealing animal.

"Go, Dub go! Go left! Go left!"

Dub focused on his target, pulled the pig to the ground by the neck and hooked his back legs around the animal's torso.

"With a time of forty-five seconds, and the time to beat, Big Heart Ranch's own Dub Lewis!"

Dub raced out of the arena and into Jack's arms. "Jack, I'm the time to beat!"

Jack offered a high-five. "Whoa, that's some grease on you, pal."

"Stewie and Henry are going now."

They stood side by side at the fence, hands gripping the rail as each competitor had their moment of glory in the ring with the pig. Lucy, too, cheered her buddies from the sidelines.

"And the winner of the junior greased pig competition, with a time of forty-five seconds, is Dub Lewis."

Dub's eyes rounded, and he started to jump up and down. "Jack. Jack. I won!"

"Yahoo!" Jack shouted. He scooped Dub up and raced him through the applauding crowd to the winner's circle to get his ribbon.

"That was great, guys," Lucy said. She mussed Dub's hair. "I am so proud of you."

Dub held his ribbon up for her to examine. "Look, Miss Lucy. Mr. Jack told me how to grab the pig, and it worked."

"Oh, Dub. Wait until your sisters see this."

"Do you know where my sissies are, Miss Lucy?"

"They're with Miss Lorna at the line dance competition. We'll find them later. Don't worry."

"Dub, let's pin this on your shirt," Jack said as

he wiped his hands on his jeans. He knelt down next to Dub and grabbed a wad of fabric, but the ribbon kept dangling crooked.

Lucy knelt next to him. "Let me help."

Their hands touched as she took the ribbon and expertly attached it to Dub's shirt. Lucy's gaze met his and she smiled, a soft, smile that reached her eyes and warmed him inside and out.

"Thank you, Lucy," Jack murmured.

"You're very welcome."

He stood. "Which way is the food? Us cowboys need to eat after a hard day tackling greased pigs."

"Follow your nose," Lucy said.

"Left."

"Correct." Lucy grabbed his arm. "Look, Jack."

He turned in time to see a vintage red humpback Chevy pickup truck pull into the parking lot.

"It's exactly the same as my dad's."

"Wow, she's a beauty. Do you recognize the driver? An alumni?"

"Let me go check." A moment later she returned with a smile on her face. "He's the husband of an alumni and he restores cars." She waved a business card. "I've got his number. I'm going to stop by and take the Chevy for a test drive."

"Way to go, Lucy. I'm proud of you."

"What for?" she asked.

"For doing something for Lucy, for a change." He smiled, sharing her enthusiasm. "So you're getting rid of the Honda?"

"Old Yeller? Yes, I'm warming to the idea." She grinned and looked back at the truck. "A test drive, Jack. That's all."

"Can we get our food now?" Dub asked.

"Single-minded, aren't you, Dub? I guess that's what makes a greased pig champion." Jack pointed to a picnic table in view of the Chevy. "I'll grab the food. Why don't you and Miss Lucy wait here?"

"Burger for me, please," Lucy said.

"Me, too," Dub chimed in.

When Jack returned to the bench, Dub was asleep with his head on Lucy's lap.

"He's beat. No mutton busting for this little guy." Lucy smoothed back the hair from Dub's forehead. "Lorna said he's been having trouble sleeping again."

"Again?" Jack sat down on the other side of Dub and placed the food on the picnic table.

"Yes. He couldn't sleep when he first came to Big Heart Ranch."

"What's going on now?"

"Dub knows the end of summer is almost here. He's worried. For himself and his sisters."

Moisture welled in Lucy's eyes. She bit her lip and stared ahead. "No child should have to worry like that. Dub Lewis has grown-up problems, and it's not fair. A little boy shouldn't have to sacrifice his childhood to protect his sisters."

A sucker punch hit Jack straight in the gut as a lone tear rolled down Lucy's cheek.

"What can I do to make sure the fostering goes through for you, Lucy? Whatever you need. I'm your guy."

"Pray, Jack. Pray."

He could do that. The Lord had given him plenty of practice this summer at Big Heart Ranch. He'd developed a proficiency for stall mucking, coop cleaning and prayer. Time to put that last one to work.

# Chapter Twelve

"Here you go, Iris. Two Big Heart Ranch staff T-shirts. Jeans or slacks are the uniform. No sneakers, and absolutely no open-toed shoes. This is a working ranch and you could be called out into the field at a moment's notice, so keep a pair of boots at the office."

"Yes, Ms. Maxwell," the young woman replied with a nod.

"Call me Lucy."

"Yes, ma'am. Um, Jack said I'd have my own office."

"Of course he did." Lucy laughed. This was yet another one of those "oh, that Jack" moments she was learning to take in stride.

Lucy opened the door to the supply closet. "Unfortunately, until Jack builds you an office from pixie dust, we're going to have to be creative." She shoved the copier against the wall with her hip and propped open the door.

"Do I have a phone?"

"Yes. I would have ordered you one sooner, however, *someone* failed to let me know you'd be starting today. He told me Monday. The phone company technicians promised that an installer is on his way. Make sure they give you a jack in here, along with your cable connection. Oh, and the guy who does our computers is coming this afternoon."

Iris glanced at the boxed computer on the floor. "Oh, I can take care of the computer. All your tech will need to do is download the software."

"Really?"

"Consider it done."

"Terrific."

"Would it be okay to reorganize this room?"

"Of course. Make it your own. There's a closet down the hall and a conference room. Anything you can discreetly move into either of those locations is fine with me."

"Thank you, Lucy."

"No. Thank you, Iris. Despite my lack of preparation for your first day, and the fact that this is Friday and my brain already checked out, I'm excited you're here. One glance into my office will verify that. I have a ton of work to dump on you." She smiled. "Of course, I mean that in the nicest possible way."

Iris chuckled, and Lucy was certain that despite her misgivings, things were going to work out. If Iris relieved Lucy of the day-to-day stressors of the office, then Jack would be proven right. She did need an admin.

"Thank you, Jack," she whispered.

Rue had a point—she did need to learn to allow people to help her, without being afraid.

Was partnering with Jack to review the ranch funding such a bad idea? She hadn't reevaluated the expenditures in five years. Sure, they'd hired an independent auditor each year, but those results simply kept the books in order. Suddenly the idea of her and Jack working together held an exciting appeal.

Lucy's desk phone rang the moment she sat down. Soon someone else would be handling these calls. She glanced at the ivy on the windowsill. Perhaps Iris could resuscitate the plant, as well.

She pushed the stack of fostering paperwork ready for the Department of Human Services aside and picked up the phone.

"Lucy Maxwell, Big Heart Ranch."

"Ms. Maxwell, this is Asa Morgan with Morgan and Masters in Manhattan. I'm trying to reach Jackson Harris. The numbers we have on file for him aren't functional and his aunt referred me to you. I understand Mr. Harris is doing pro bono work with your ranch this summer."

Emma peeked her head in, and Lucy put her hand over the receiver.

"Lucy, I'm leaving for court," she whispered. "The judge requested my presence. There's a juvenile that they'd like to place at the ranch. I gave Iris my phone number in case something comes up."

Lucy nodded and returned her attention to the

phone call. "Yes. Mr. Harris is with us. I'm pulling up his schedule right now. Please bear with me. Ah, yes, he's with Mrs. Carmody right now."

"Oh, I don't want to take him away from a client. Could you have him return my call as soon as possible? We're hoping to get him out to New York immediately."

"I will give him the message."

"Off the record, Ms. Maxwell, we've heard some very good things about his activities in the nonprofit sector. Could you comment, as his employer this summer?"

"Mr. Morgan, you know that employment law forbids me from confirming or denying anything, except to say that Mr. Harris is indeed here at Big Heart Ranch for the summer."

He chuckled. "Right. Forget I even asked."

"Forgotten. I'll have Mr. Harris call you back immediately."

"Thank you."

Lucy put the phone down and stared at the calendar in stunned silence as the conversation she'd just had sank in.

"Oklahoma has grown on him, huh?" she said aloud. She should have known he'd last about as long as his worthless promise to volunteer through the end of summer.

What did she expect? The silly thing was that she should have seen this one coming in a

Brooks Brothers suit, and a mile away, too, despite his kisses.

Or maybe she meant in spite of them.

Lucy swallowed and bowed her head. Every single red flag was there. Yet she'd let herself believe that Jack Harris really did care about her. That his kisses meant something.

What about Dub and the ranch? Did he care about them?

"This isn't personal, Lucy," she whispered. "Jack Harris is a temporary cowboy here on an assignment for the Brisbane Foundation. That's what he said, and that's exactly what he's doing."

If she'd been fooled, it was her own fault.

"Lucy? Am I interrupting?"

When she looked up, Iris stood hesitantly on the threshold of Lucy's office.

"I was talking to myself. I should have warned you about that."

Iris hesitated.

"Come on in. I know it looks terrifying in here, but really, it's harmless."

"Um, your sister called to ask if you authorized a moving truck."

"A truck?"

"Roscoe from USA Rentals. He was apparently lost and she directed him to the lodge."

"The lodge?" Lucy blinked, a knot forming in her stomach. "You're sure he went to the lodge?"

"Yes, ma'am."

Lucy stood. "I'm going to check on this. I'll need you to listen for the front door and take messages if anyone stops by. Don't worry about the phones." She paused and offered a grimace. "Can you handle all that? This is your first day, and I don't want to overwhelm you."

"Ma'am, I've got everything under control."

"Control," Lucy murmured. "Control is a good thing." She headed out the door of her office and backtracked. "The forms! Could you please get this paperwork mailed to the Department of Human Services? It needs to be taken directly to the post office and overnighted."

"Yes, ma'am."

"Thank you, Iris. When I get back, we'll work on that ma'am stuff. It makes me feel like your grandmother."

"Yes…okay, Lucy."

Lucy got into the Honda and turned the key. The car sputtered and coughed but refused to turn over. She put a gentle hand on the dashboard. "You're upset because I looked at that pickup truck, aren't you? I'm sorry."

She tried the ignition again. Not even a click this time. With a groan, she got out of the car and headed to the stables.

Riding to the lodge was the only solution. Lucy picked up speed, finally breaking into a run until she reached the open doors of the stables. Catching her breath, she checked the schedule.

Blaze was free. After a hurried tack up, she offered the gelding feed before they took off. "Blaze, we're going to take a shortcut through the woods. I'm going to need you to cooperate."

The moving truck pulled up to the turnoff to the lodge just as Lucy cleared the woods. Her eyes widened with surprise at the professional sign at the entrance to the lodge. Though she sat on Blaze, positioned at an angle, she could still see the lettering on the sign.

Big Heart Ranch Retreat Center had been burned into its wooden archway. The truck barely cleared the sign as it chugged slowly up to the log cabin house.

Lucy clicked her tongue and nudged Blaze forward, as well. She slid off the gelding's back and tied the reins in a clove hitch around the horse post outside the stables.

All the while, her gaze was focused on the lodge. She walked toward the log cabin house with measured steps. The change took her breath away. It was as she had imagined a lifetime ago when she'd bought the place.

The windows held boxes that overflowed with red and white geraniums. Huge clay pots stood guard at either side of the front door and were filled with more flowers and elephant ear plants. The porch held hanging pots of massive Boston ferns.

Red Adirondack chairs and footstools had been

placed casually on the porch and under the willow tree and welcomed a seat in the shade.

*Almost ready for his presentation?* That's what he'd said. She hitched a breath and swallowed hard.

"I need your signature."

Lucy whirled around. "Excuse me?"

"I need your signature on this load." A stout man pulled a pen from his uniform pocket and tapped on his clipboard.

"No, I'm afraid I don't know anything about a load."

"Jack Harris around? He was supposed to meet me here."

"Then I'm sure he'll be along."

She strode toward the house.

"Lady, time is money."

"I'm sure it is, Roscoe, and you can bill Mr. Harris. This is his problem. Not mine."

Keys. She'd given Jack her keys. Then she remembered the emergency key in a fake rock under the massive redbud in the front yard. Three years ago she had put that key in the rock and buried it.

On her knees, she searched the base of the tree until she located the spot. After three years, the rock had sunk into the red clay and was now practically embedded into the ground. She used her car key to dig it up. At least Old Yeller was still good for something. Sitting on her haunches, Lucy pulled the rock from the ground and opened the shell case.

She grinned and held up the key.

The mat outside the front door had been engraved with the words Welcome to Big Heart Ranch Retreat Center.

"All the personal touches, right, Jack? No wonder this took you so long. You weren't planning a presentation—you planned a done deal. So much for working together. For partnerships." She released a groan of frustration.

Lucy stood at the threshold, a hand on the knob and the key in the lock, though her feet seemed unable to move. Overwhelmed, she closed her eyes and slowly inhaled.

Last night she'd tossed and turned thinking about Jack Harris and his kisses. She realized with stunning wonder that she was falling in love. Not with the attorney, but with the volunteer who had replaced Leo and stolen her heart. And she actually liked the idea. A lot.

But that was last night. This was now.

Fear paralyzed her for a few moments. Finally, she turned the knob and pushed the door open.

A small and elegant reception desk faced the door, surrounded by baskets of overflowing ferns and ivy. On the desk, another basket held menus to local eateries that delivered. Yet another held mints with the ranch name and number on black-and-gold wrappers.

The once-empty main living room behind the desk had been converted into a stylish cross between a hotel lobby and a real lodge. Cozy seating arrangements were placed around the room, along with an internet charging table. Jack had brought high-speed internet to the lodge. Of course—if it could be done, Jack was the man to do it. No amenities had been spared.

The fireplace had stacks of wood on either side. Over the mantel, a reproduction of a Bob Timberlake painting that depicted a ranch in winter hung. Mesmerized, she stared at the painting.

Lucy wandered into the kitchen next. Shiny pots and pans hung over the center island. Unable to resist, she opened cupboards and drawers. Dishes, silver and even thick kitchen towels filled the drawers.

Her suspicions were verified. Jack Harris had never planned to propose a facility at the lodge. He'd forged ahead and created something beyond her imagination. The place was amazing. He was not a man of half measures. The evolution of this house from empty to visionary revealed the real Jackson Harris. A man who went after what he wanted, no matter the cost.

How had she not seen this coming?

Her closet.

Lucy willed her heart to stop pounding so hard. She stared at the pantry closet for moments, grappling with her emotions. Her hands trembled as she remembered sharing the painful secrets with Jack in there. The memory burned, and she held her hands to her flushed face.

Twisting the knob, she realized the pantry was unlocked. Lucy slowly opened the door and turned on the light. Nothing had been touched. It remained as it was the last time she was there. With Jack.

Lucy put a hand on her heart and realized it was beating overtime, and her breath was coming in shallow pants. Hyperventilating again. She leaned over, hands on her knees, and willed herself to relax.

From the other room, the sound of the front door opening and footsteps echoing on the pine floor filled the silence. She turned her head in time to see Jack step into the kitchen with a smile on his face.

Their gazes connected, and the smile faded.

"Lucy, what are you doing here? I didn't see Old Yeller."

"I rode Blaze."

"This was supposed to be a surprise."

She sucked in a shaky breath. "Surprise!"

He stepped closer. "I can explain."

The time for explanations was long past. About four weeks too long. Lucy struggled to keep her voice calm.

"What's in the moving truck, Jack?"

"More furniture."

"More?" She nodded, thoughtfully considering that one word.

"For the upstairs rooms."

"You bought furniture, too?"

"No. My aunt had furniture in the stables. I figured upcycling was a good thing."

"That's green of you."

The awkward silence was broken when Roscoe came in carrying a rocking chair.

"Where do you want this stuff?"

"Put everything in the bedrooms upstairs," Jack directed.

"There was a call for you," Lucy said when Roscoe left the room. "Asa Morgan with Morgan and Masters in Manhattan. He's very impressed with what he's heard about your nonprofit work."

She stared at him, trying to figure out who Jack Harris really was. How had she been so easily duped?

"Is that all we are at Big Heart Ranch, Jack? An opportunity for you to build your résumé, sharpen your skill set?"

"What do you want me to say, Lucy?"

"I want you to say that you really do care about Dub. That you believe our ranch is the real thing, and that the last few weeks haven't been simply a chance for you to explore your entrepreneurial side at our expense before you head back to New York."

"They're courting me. I didn't reach out to

them. Summer is almost over. The fact is, I have to make some hard decisions soon."

She bowed her head.

"Whatever you think I've done, you're wrong." He shrugged. "But you've already convicted me. Right, Lucy?"

"Why did you lead me to believe you were busy drawing up plans and proposals all this time?"

"I had to work around the fact that you keep your expectations low. That you weren't ready to move on."

Lucy met his gaze. "What does that mean?"

"It means that you can't let go of the past long enough to see the future. Telling you about the future wasn't going to work. I knew I had to show it to you. Show you possibilities, or you'd continue to define this house as your epic failure."

"It is my failure."

He shook his head. "Lucy, you've taught me so much about second chances. About leaving the past behind. Why is it you give everyone a second chance but yourself? This house is not a failure. It's a possibility, just like your kids. Maybe even like us."

"Us? There is no us. You lied to me."

"I didn't lie. I dodged the truth. If I'm guilty of anything, it's caring too much. I suggested working together, but you wouldn't even hear that option. I made a decision to work around you, in an effort to get through to you." He ran a hand through his hair. "My aunt tried to warn me that this wasn't the right approach. I didn't listen to her."

"How did you fund..." She waved an arm around the room. "All of this?"

"Consider it a donation from a private donor. Me. Not my aunt."

"Thank you for not touching my closet," she murmured.

"You're the only one who can empty that closet."

A phone began to ring, and Lucy reached into her back pocket and pulled it out. "Sure, Iris. I'll be right there." Lucy headed for the door.

"Where does this leave us, Lucy?" Jack asked.

"The same place we were five weeks ago. I represent the children of Big Heart Ranch and implore you to approve the donation funds."

"What about us?" he pressed.

"Seriously, Jack? Relationships are messy and complicated, and they take time and dedication. You can't plan them out on one of your spreadsheets. Your money can't buy love." She turned away. "I'm sorry you don't get that."

Jack blinked, his eyes gritty from lack of sleep. He led Zeus from his stall out to the pen. The horse offered an agitated whinny on principle.

"Don't you start on me, too." Jack grabbed the shovel. The cowboy's cure for insomnia. He started mucking with a vengeance. Stall by stall, and in under a few hours the stables were cleaner than even the amazing Leo could have produced.

Leo. Maybe he should give the guy a call and see if he'd consider a raise to return to Big Heart Ranch. He felt guilty leaving the ranch in the lurch. Jack pulled off a glove and made a note on his phone.

"Jack, just the man I want to see."

He raised his head and narrowed his eyes at General Rue Butterfield, who stood in the middle of the stables.

"Normally those are exactly the words I want to hear. Today, not so much."

"What happened between you and Lucy?"

"Nothing. A big fat nothing."

Rue sighed and put her arms on top of the stall gate. "Jack, I never figured you for a coward."

"I'm not."

"Let's pretend for a moment that those words are true."

Jack raised a brow.

"What about the ranch funding?" she asked.

"Signed on Friday, General. The certified check should be on the director's desk..." He glanced at his watch. "What day is it? Time flies when you spend your time banging your head against a wall."

"Wednesday."

"I met with the accountant yesterday. It will be on Miss Maxwell's desk tomorrow afternoon."

"That's a relief."

He couldn't think of a single satisfying response, so he pulled on his glove and stabbed at the straw with the pitchfork.

"Less than two weeks left. You're staying until the end of summer?" Rue asked.

"I always keep my word."

"Good to know. What about the gala?"

"That's my aunt's department. I'd rather get tossed off Zeus than attend another party."

"What will you do once the summer is over?"

"I couldn't tell you."

"You're going to walk away?"

"I've examined this situation carefully. I don't see that I have any choice."

"Let me get this straight. You'd rather walk away from the possibility of everything and jump straight into a future that holds nothing than fight for what you want."

He looked at her. "Admittedly, when you say it like that, it doesn't sound too smart."

Rue laughed. "At least your sense of humor is still intact."

"Always."

"Mr. Jack?" Dub stuck his head around the corner. "Are we having lessons this week?"

"Yeah. Right on schedule, tomorrow afternoon at three."

Dub pulled a shiny quarter from his pocket and held it out to the general.

"What's that you have, Dub?" she asked.

"A quarter. Mr. Jack said I can keep it." Dub cocked his head and watched Jack. "You okay, Mr. Jack? You're not getting sick, are you?"

"I'm good, Dub."

Dub turned and walked out of the barn, tossing the quarter in the air and catching it again as he went.

Jack winced. He was getting sick all right. The thought of leaving Dub behind turned his stomach.

"He's in tune to you, Jack."

"What does that mean?"

"It means he knows something is up." Rue shook her head. "Sadly, Dub is the one who's going to suffer when you walk away."

"There's nothing I can do to fix things. Lucy's happy to see me leave. She thinks I'm heavy-handed and dishonest."

"Are you?"

"My intentions were honorable. But yeah, I messed up. Big time. What can I do, General?"

"I don't know, but I'm sure you'll think of something, because come ten days from now you won't be the only one in a world of hurt."

Jack swallowed hard as Rue left the barn. He'd come to Big Heart Ranch an empty man. If he left things as they were, he'd be walking away exactly the same. Somehow he had to find a way to get Lucy to forgive him, because he wasn't willing to turn his back on everything he loved.

# Chapter Thirteen

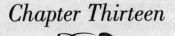

"This arrived by courier, Lucy."

Lucy looked up from her desk at the official-looking envelope Iris held out to her.

"By courier? We're twenty minutes from Timber, Oklahoma. Who sends things by courier?"

A frown crossed the admin's face. "Is that rhetorical?"

"Yes." Lucy cleared a place on her desk, which she noted was significantly less messy since Iris had started last Friday. Another thing to thank Jack for.

"Don't you want it?"

Lucy pointed to the spot she'd cleared, and Iris dropped the envelope on the desk.

"Oh, and General Butterfield called and asked for a few minutes of your time. However, she didn't wait for an answer. She's on her way over."

"I always have an open door for the general."

Iris nodded. "Do you mind if I run some errands for Emma tomorrow morning? She's swamped with preparations for the gala."

"Of course. Thank you for being so flexible, Iris."

"I like it here, Lucy. I don't have any family. Big Heart Ranch sort of feels like home."

"I'm glad to hear that."

Lucy stared at the envelope. The embossed return address was from the Brisbane Foundation Legal Department. That would be attorney Jackson Harris's department.

He was everywhere.

A shiver raced over her. She clenched and unclenched her hands, knowing that the future of Big Heart Ranch was inside an unremarkable white envelope delivered by courier on a Thursday in August.

She'd been asking around, and though she hadn't run into him since last Friday, as far as she could tell, Jack was still living at the bunkhouse. According to a little surreptitious checking, she'd learned that he continued to fulfill his promise to stay at the ranch through the end of summer and fill Leo's shoes.

Lucy rubbed her forehead. How had things gotten so out of control so quickly? She glanced at the red-team ball cap sitting on her bookcase and smiled, remembering Jack yelling at her to slide into home at the ball game. Jack and Dub laughing as they created monster ice cream sundaes together. That wonderful kiss at the soiree when she was naive enough to think she might be falling in love with Jack.

Soon it would all be a memory, tucked away like a pressed flower.

Eight more days until the gala. The gala was

supposed to be a jubilant time when they celebrated the year's blessings. Another year of mending broken hearts and providing second chances.

What about Dub? His little heart would be broken when he and his sisters went back to the Pawhuska Children's Orphanage.

Though it was ridiculously too soon to expect a response, Lucy pulled up her email to verify no one had contacted her from DHS about the foster program.

She released a dramatic sigh and held the envelope to her desk lamp.

"Aren't you going to open it?"

She looked up at Rue, then put the envelope on the desk and folded her hands over the top. "I haven't decided."

"Come on, Lucy, open the letter."

"I'm not sure I'm ready for what's inside."

"Everywhere I go on this ranch, folks are dancing to the same tune."

"Okay, I'll bite. What tune would that be?"

"The chicken dance."

Lucy chuckled. "Does this mean you've stopped by to share some sage wisdom with me?"

"Whenever I can. You don't get to be my age without learning a thing or two. Usually the hard way." Rue shook her head. "If I can save some folks the heartache I suffered needlessly due to my own pigheadedness, then by golly, I'm going to try."

"I'm sure there's a lesson in there somewhere."

"Open the envelope. That's the lesson for the day."

Lucy took the letter opener from her drawer, slid the point beneath the letter's gummed flap and sliced the envelope. The check fluttered to the desk.

Lucy slowly reached out and turned it over. She trembled as she read the amount.

"This is the largest donation to the ranch that we have ever received from the Brisbane Foundation," she whispered. "It's more than we requested."

"Isn't God good?"

"Wait until Travis and Emma find out." Lucy put a hand to her heart in a futile effort to slow its wild beating. "Oh, my goodness. I'm speechless."

"You deserve this, Lucy. You've worked hard for that check."

"Yet I'm humbled. I had moments when I doubted the Lord and even whined a bit. I definitely have time on my knees in my immediate future."

"Do you think you can handle more good news?" Rue's eyes twinkled.

"I'm not sure." Lucy blinked and cocked her head. "What are you up to?"

"I made a few phone calls, and your fostering paperwork has been expedited."

"What does that mean?"

"It means you've been selected to foster Dub, Ann and Eva, pending inspection of your domicile and, of course, approval of the children."

"Rue, I live in a one-bedroom apartment."

"It's okay. DHS understands. The children will stay in their homes on the ranch until you locate a place suitable for all of you."

"How did you do this?" Moisture blurred her vision as she spoke.

"There's really not much point in being a general if you can't pull in favors every now and again." She shrugged. "It's always good to have friends in high places."

Lucy stood up and came around the desk to hug her friend. "Oh, Rue. That little boy and his sisters are going to get the second chance they deserve."

Rue wiped her own eyes. "I promised myself I wouldn't blubber."

Lucy sniffed and handed the older woman a tissue.

"The hard part is going to be up to you," Rue said.

"You mean talking to the children?" Lucy paused before she sat down. "You're right. What if they don't want me to be their foster parent?"

"Get real, Lucy. Those kids love you."

"What hard part are you referring to?"

"You have to talk to Jack."

"Jack?"

"Don't leave him out of this. He recommended

the increased funding, and he's your biggest cheerleader. I know for a fact that he and his aunt also spoke to the DHS regarding you fostering."

"They did?"

"Yes."

"How do you know all this?"

Rue shrugged and glanced at the calendar. "Don't make the mistake of thinking you have all the time in the world to make this right, Lucy. You don't."

"There's a lot of hurt between Jack and me. I don't know if I can bridge that. Besides, he has job offers in New York City."

"He's still here. It doesn't seem to me that he's in any rush to leave. Jack will stay in Oklahoma if you ask him. Deep down inside, he wants you to ask him. He longs to be part of something that's forever, just like you do."

Lucy was silent, overwhelmed by Rue's observations.

"Second chances are great, Lucy, until you miss the window of opportunity."

"Are you suggesting I beg him to stay?"

"No, I'm suggesting that you tell him how you feel."

"I don't think I can," Lucy murmured.

"I think you better. You can't afford to leave things unsaid." She smiled sadly at Lucy. "You of all people should have learned this long ago."

"What if he doesn't... What if he says no?"

"You can't lose until you saddle up and try."

"Okay, Rue. When the time is right, I'll talk to Jack."

"I know I can count on you," Rue said.

Iris appeared in the doorway. "I'm so sorry to interrupt, but Lorna has been trying to reach you on your cell, Lucy. She says it's urgent. Dub Lewis is missing."

Adrenaline shot through Lucy. She grabbed her purse. "Rue, can you head over to the security office and ask them to check the cameras? I'll phone you when I have details."

"Of course."

"Jack. I have to find Jack." Lucy jumped into the Ute and put her phone on speaker, hitting the auto dial button over and over.

Jack Harris wasn't picking up.

"What?" Jack sat straight up in bed.

The banging at the bunkhouse door had him scrambling for his phone.

Six p.m. He'd fallen asleep for four hours?

The banging didn't let up.

He pulled open the door, nearly knocking the ranch director off her feet. "Lucy? What's wrong?"

"Dub is missing."

"Missing?" Jack struggled to breathe. Realization hit him like a solid punch in the gut. "I missed his riding lesson. I fell asleep."

"What time was the lesson scheduled?"

"Three," he groaned.

"Lorna went to check on him when he didn't come down for dinner. He wasn't in his room."

"What about his house brothers?"

"Stewie and Henry don't know anything. But his bicycle is still in the garage."

"Is he with his sisters?"

"No, she already called over there."

"We can take my car," Jack offered.

"Jack, it'll be better if we split up. You check the boys' ranch. I'll go to the girls' ranch and look around. Rue is working with security."

He grabbed his boots and shoved his feet into them. "This should have never happened, Lucy. That kid has way too much freedom."

She grimaced and turned away. "Please, don't play the blame game, Jack. Not now. I love that little boy as much as you do. I'm planning my future around him."

"Then why did he leave?"

"Why do you think? Dub is smart. He knows summer is over in a week. And he knows you're leaving. You missing that lesson today must have had him in a panic that you were already gone."

"It's my fault."

"Stop. Focus on Dub. We'll find him."

"All it takes is one moment, and your life changes forever."

Lucy's face paled at his words.

"We have to find Dub," Jack said, fighting emotions that threatened to paralyze him.

"You're right, Jack. We both understand that only too well. But this isn't about you or me. This is about a hurting child who is afraid he's going to lose everything once again. This is the time for prayers, not accusations or self-recrimination."

She walked out the front door without looking back.

Jack grabbed his keys and got in the Lexus. His thoughts flashed back to his brother, and for the first time in twenty-five years he once again felt the sinking despair of helplessness pressing down. He couldn't lose someone he loved again. Not like this.

"Dub, where are you?" Jack rested his head on the steering wheel and began to pray. "Lord, that boy means more to me than I realized. Help me find him. Help me make things right."

For several minutes, Jack stared out the windshield at the ranch where activities were winding down around him.

*The loft.*

Dub would be in the loft if he was anywhere.

Jack started the car and headed to the stables.

The front door stood open as children and staff finished grooming their horses for the day. Jack walked to the end of the building. Tripp's office was dark. Outside Grace's stall, something shiny winked at him. He crouched down and scattered the straw, uncovering a quarter.

Grace whinnied and nodded. She shook her head toward the loft overhead. "Thanks, Grace," Jack whispered, rubbing the mare's ears.

He took the back stairs and nearly stumbled over the sleeping child at the top.

"Dub," Jack whispered, his relief raw.

Dub had neatly placed Grace's pad on the ground and lay on the flannel, curled on his side, his hands tucked beneath his head, quietly sleeping. Tear tracks had dried on his dusty face.

The five-year-old had been crying.

Jack closed his eyes and ran a hand over his own face. "I'm sorry, Dub."

He eased down to the loft floor next to Dub. For minutes he simply watched the child sleep. Swiping at his eyes with the back of his hands, Jack released a silent prayer of thanks.

"What am I going to do, Lord?" he whispered. "I can't leave this boy."

Dub's eyes fluttered open. "Mr. Jack?" A small smile crossed his face.

"Yes, Dub."

"I thought you were gone. Stewie and Henry said you were going away. You didn't come for my lesson."

"That was an accident, Dub. I'm so sorry. I fell asleep."

"You're here now."

"Yes, but you're right—I'm leaving when the summer is over. I have a few more days."

"I'm going back to the orphanage," Dub said as he sat up. "My sissies, too."

Jack nodded.

Dub twisted his hands in his lap. "I thought if I prayed hard, God would hear, and me and my sissies could stay at the ranch."

"Oh, Dub. I know God is listening. Sometimes things don't happen when we think they should, but He always hears our prayers."

"I wish He'd hurry up."

"Me, too."

"What about Grace?" Dub frowned as if in pain. "Who will take care of Grace? She needs her carrots, and her ears rubbed. She'll be sad if you and me both go away, Mr. Jack."

"Mr. Tripp takes good care of all the horses. Don't worry about Grace."

Dub gave a resigned nod.

"Miss Lorna and Miss Lucy are worried about you, Dub. You missed dinner."

"I'm thorry." Dub grabbed the flannel pad and stood up. He shook the straw from the fabric.

"I'll take care of that later. Are you hungry?"

"No." Dub stared at the stables stretched out before him, then finally looked up at Jack, his lower lip quivering. "I don't want to leave the ranch. It's like a real home."

"I know, Dub. I don't want to leave, either."

"Maybe Miss Lucy will let us stay. We can ask her, can't we?"

Lucy's words came back to him. *Don't make promises you can't keep.* Jack's lips were a thin line as he looked at his buddy without offering him the promises he desperately needed to hear.

Dub nodded. "It's okay. Don't be sad, Mr. Jack. I know sometimes we gots to follow the rules."

Jack choked on the emotions overwhelming him. Without thinking, he scooped the little boy up in his arms. "I love you, buddy."

Dub Lewis tucked his head into Jack's chest. "I love you, too, Mr. Jack."

# Chapter Fourteen

Lucy saddled Blaze and led her out into the sunshine. She'd checked Jack's schedule before she snuck into the stables. He'd be in the chicken coops for at least another hour. This would be as good a time as any to take the shortcut to the lodge and empty that closet. She might figure out what to do about Jack Harris while she was cleaning up her life.

As she approached the house, she was once again struck by the transformation. The place welcomed visitors. Encouraged them to sit on the porch or rest beneath the willow tree.

Jack was right. It made sense to use the lodge to support the ranch. She'd been stubborn on principle, and he'd been high-handed. The two of them were quite a pair. Controlling to the bitter end, and where had it gotten either of them?

Control had served her well when she was a foster child looking after Travis and Emma. She was a long way from those days. With a glance at her hands, Lucy opened the palms. "I'm finally giving it all to You, Lord."

Lucy had barely unlocked the front door and walked in when the doorbell rang. She turned to discover Meredith Brisbane on the porch, carrying an enormous bouquet of long-stemmed sunflowers, wrapped in green floral paper.

"Meredith?" Lucy looked past the elegant matriarch to the limousine parked outside the lodge.

"Hello, Lucy. Your assistant told me you'd be here."

Lucy opened the screen, and Meredith handed her the bouquet. "My nephew once said that sunflowers reminded him of you."

She did a double take at the words. *Jack said that?*

"They're lovely." Lucy fingered the bright yellow petals. "What are they for?"

"Your foster request was approved."

"Yes, it was. Thank you so much for putting in a good word for me."

"I adore those children. So does Jackson. We both know you'll be a wonderful mother."

"A mother." The words rolled off her tongue, and she paused to consider them, sinking down into a chair. "Things have been so incredibly busy that I hadn't even stopped to think about that. I'll be someone's mom. Wow."

"I'd say a few wows are in order."

"Come on in, Meredith. Let me put these in water." She stood and headed to the kitchen. Suddenly Lucy stopped and turned. "Where's your cane?"

Jack's aunt held up her empty hands. "I'm feeling so much better. No cane needed."

"That's wonderful."

Lucy led Meredith into the kitchen and searched the cupboards for a large vase, but came up empty. "Excuse me a moment."

Second shelf on the right. Tucked near the back. Exactly where she'd put it three years ago. Lucy opened the pantry door and carefully removed the vase from the original gift box. She placed the crystal cylinder in the sink under running water.

"This is your house?" Meredith asked, her gaze sweeping the open spaces and high ceilings.

"Yes. I bought the place a long time ago. It's been empty ever since."

"Why has this house come between you and Jackson?"

Lucy took a deep breath, turned off the faucet and faced Meredith. "I could tell you that he and I have had differing views on the future of the ranch, and this house. But the truth would be because we're both bossy and pigheaded."

"That's a shame." Meredith stepped into the open living room. "So this is where he brought all that furniture." She walked across the room and stood in front of the fireplace to admire the painting. "Bob Timberlake. It looks like a first edition print."

"Is it? I don't even know where it came from," Lucy admitted.

"Oh, Jackson, I imagine."

Lucy's gaze followed Meredith's. As she glanced

around, she realized how nicely the furniture and accessories fit in the lodge. It was almost as though they were supposed to be there.

"Lucy, did you see the chandelier in the great room at the estate?"

"Yes. It's incredible. The heart-shaped crystals."

"My husband bought it for me because he had it in his head that the chandelier was something I longed for." She smiled serenely. "I didn't really. However, every time I look at that chandelier and see the prisms of light reflected from those hearts I remember how much he loved me. That chandelier was his expression of love."

Lucy was silent as Meredith continued.

"Have you ever considered that what my nephew did with this house is his expression of love?"

Lucy's eyes widened.

"Jackson knew right away that you weren't a crook, and that Big Heart Ranch was legitimate. He respected and admired your steadfast devotion to the ministry God gave you." Meredith laughed. "He's been more than a little perturbed that you care more about his stall-mucking ability than his bank account or his family ties."

"I don't understand. Then why didn't he sign the paperwork?"

"I asked him the same thing that day when you were at the house with the children. He said that if he signed it on week two, he wouldn't have a reason to stay at the ranch for the summer. Jackson cared for you right from the beginning." She smiled again. "He was determined to make sure you'd never lose Big Heart Ranch. I believe he said something about a Plan B."

Lucy's jaw sagged at the words.

"My nephew loves you."

"He certainly has a funny way of showing it."

"Oh, don't get me wrong. He was completely in the wrong. I told him that from the start. He made a mistake."

Meredith stepped closer and took Lucy's hands. "I've grown to love you as well, Lucy. You're an amazing woman. It would be my dearest wish if you could find it in your heart to forgive Jackson. To give him a second chance. Do you think you can do that?"

Emotion stinging her eyes, Lucy nodded.

"What are you doing?" Jack asked. He assessed the boxes spread over the kitchen floor. Lucy Maxwell was on the closet floor, with her boots sticking out into the kitchen of the lodge.

She jerked when he spoke, and the sound of her head connecting with a shelf echoed in the kitchen. "Ouch."

Jack groaned. "Sorry. I didn't mean to surprise you."

Lucy crawled out of the closet and looked up at him. "What does it look like I'm doing?"

He opened his mouth and then closed it, determined not to make a mess of things today. *Focus, Jack.* The reason he was here was to fix what he'd already messed up.

When she dusted off her jeans and began to stand, Jack quickly offered her a hand.

"Thanks. I was getting a little stiff." Their gazes connected, and she paused, glancing down at her hand in his before stepping back.

"Dust bunny at twelve o'clock," he said.

"Huh?"

Jack plucked a ball of dust from her hair and offered it to her. Lucy laughed when he placed it in her palm.

He smiled. Lucy laughing was a very good sign.

"So you were saying?"

"Saying?" Lucy frowned, confused.

"The closet."

"Oh, that." Lucy gestured with a hand. "I'm moving on with my life." She picked up a stack of small boxes and put them on the kitchen island. "Six trivets, Jack. How many trivets does one woman need?"

He frowned. "I don't know the answer to that question."

When she laughed again, the tightness in his chest eased. Maybe this wasn't going to be as painful as he thought.

"Thank you for the check. And the flowers and the recommendation you provided to DHS." Her cheeks went pink, and she offered an embarrassed smile. "Actually, I have quite a bit to thank you for."

"You're welcome." He shoved his hands in his pockets. "Look, Lucy, I'm here to apologize. Let me do that before I put my foot in my mouth again."

"Okay," Lucy murmured.

"I steamrolled you with this whole Big Heart Ranch Retreat Center plan of mine."

"Yes. You did."

"I was an idiot. I thought I could force you to face your fears when I had no intention of facing mine until you made me." He released a breath. "I'm sorry."

"You are quite forgiven."

"Yeah?" He cocked his head. "I expected a lot more, you know…"

"Groveling?"

Jack nodded.

"Normally, I would require that."

"Oh?"

"Except I have so much to be thankful for, I'm feeling benevolent today." She paused. "And it's possible that despite your arrogant and high-handed ways, you actually did me a favor by forcing me to face my fears and let go of control."

"Um, thanks. I think." He met her gaze. "But it goes both ways. By twisting my arm, and pushing me to be a buddy to Dub, you helped me move past the guilt of my brother's death."

An awkward silence stretched between them. Jack met her gaze. "What are we going to do now?" he whispered.

Her expression was solemn as she lifted her chin and really looked at him. "I don't know."

"You're still afraid, aren't you?"

She sighed. "Well, duh. Of course I am. I'm terrified. I don't have any more closets, Jack."

"I'm not that other guy, you know. I won't ever leave you. I'm not perfect. When life gets messy and complicated, like you said it would, I won't ever disappear."

"What are you saying?"

"I'm saying that I love you, Lucy Maxwell."

Tenderness filled her eyes, followed immediately by wide-eyed panic.

"It's only been six weeks, Jack."

"Yeah. How about that? Six weeks is all it took for me to fall in love with you."

Lucy's mouth formed an O of astonishment. "You're really in love with me?"

"How could I not be? You've been turning my life upside down since day one."

"Your life? What about mine? I now have an admin and a guest ranch. With the new budget, we'll be able to add a few more houses to the boys' and girls' ranches. That means we can help a few more kids. Thanks to you."

"Don't give me the credit." Jack aimed his thumb heavenward. "I've been asleep for twenty-five years. He and my aunt woke me up by sending me to Big Heart Ranch. They're quite a team. They get all the credit."

Lucy gave a hesitant nod. "Yes. With a little help from the general."

"You know that this means you have to trust me. No more Plan B. No more waiting for the other boot to drop. I get that this ranch is your ministry, and that doesn't scare me."

"Maybe it should."

"Not at all. These are God's kids. This is your job. God willing, I'll partner with you in that job and at night we can go home to our children, Dub, Ann and Eva, each night."

Lucy gasped and reached for the counter as her knees wobbled. "You want to adopt them?"

Jack slipped an arm around her waist and helped her to a chair. "Of course I want to adopt them. I'd be lost without them. Without you."

"Adopt?" Lucy repeated the word. "Five hearts will get a second chance, Jack."

"A family. A forever family."

"Except I haven't even told Dub and his sisters about the foster plan yet. I haven't asked them if they want me to be their mom."

"Of course they do. But why haven't you told them?"

"I'm waiting for the official paperwork to be delivered. I can't tell them until then. What if…"

He put a finger to her mouth. "No more what-ifs, Lucy. No more zombie apocalypse backup plans."

She nodded. "You're right. You're completely right."

For a few moments, Lucy simply stared at him. Then she stood and wrapped her arms around his neck. She closed her eyes tight and opened them. "Oh, Jack," she murmured. "Who ever thought I'd fall in love with the ornery lawyer with the cute dimple?"

"I have a cute dimple?"

When she nodded, Jack lowered his head to meet her lips.

"Ah, Lucy," he breathed when they separated. "We have to get busy."

"How so?"

"We've got paperwork to file if we want to finalize the adoption in time for the wedding."

"What wedding?"

"Lucy Transparent Maxwell, will you marry me?"

"Oh, Jack," she murmured again, reaching up to kiss him. She leaned back in the circle of his arms.

"A wedding," she breathed.

"Yeah."

"With Dub and Ann and Eva."

"Is that a yes, Lucy?"

"Yes. It's a yes." She reached for a notepad on the counter. "We have so much to do. We're way behind schedule, Jack. We have to catch up and start making those forever memories for those kids. For us."

He laughed and took the paper from her. "We have a lifetime, Lucy. A lifetime for our little family."

"I love you, Jack."

"I love you too, Lucy."

* * * * *

*If you loved this story, pick up these heartwarming books from beloved author Tina Radcliffe:*

*STRANDED WITH THE RANCHER*
*SAFE IN THE FIREMAN'S ARMS*
*ROCKY MOUNTAIN REUNION*
*ROCKY MOUNTAIN COWBOY*

*Available now from Love Inspired!*

*Find more great reads at*
*www.LoveInspired.com*

Dear Reader,

Welcome to Big Heart Ranch in Timber, Oklahoma. I'm so excited about this new series. In this book and others, I'll be introducing you to the staff and kids of this ranch for orphaned, abused and neglected children, owned and operated by the orphaned Maxwell siblings, Lucy, Travis and Emma.

The first book of the series is Lucy Maxwell and Jack Harris's story. What fun it was delving into the lives of the two stubborn main characters of this book and watching God teach them how to be open to His will. Not unlike the way He does for us when we're stubborn and set in our ways. Thank You, Lord!

I hope you'll come back for more stories from Big Heart Ranch. Do drop me a note and let me know if you enjoyed this book. I can be reached through my website, www.tinaradcliffe.com.

Sincerely,
*Tina Radcliffe*

# Get 2 Free Books,
## Plus 2 Free Gifts—
### just for trying the Reader Service!

# HOMETOWN HEARTS ♥

**YES!** Please send me **The Hometown Hearts Collection** in Larger Print. This collection begins with 3 FREE books and 2 FREE gifts in the first shipment. Along with my 3 free books, I'll also get the next 4 books from the Hometown Hearts Collection, in LARGER PRINT, which I may either return and owe nothing, or keep for the low price of $4.99 U.S./ $5.89 CDN each plus $2.99 for shipping and handling per shipment*. If I decide to continue, about once a month for 8 months I will get 6 or 7 more books, but will only need to pay for 4. That means 2 or 3 books in every shipment will be FREE! If I decide to keep the entire collection, I'll have paid for only 32 books because 19 books are FREE! I understand that accepting the 3 free books and gifts places me under no obligation to buy anything. I can always return a shipment and cancel at any time. My free books and gifts are mine to keep no matter what I decide.

262 HCN 3432 462 HCN 3432

| Name | (PLEASE PRINT) | |
|------|------|------|
| Address | | Apt. # |
| City | State/Prov. | Zip/Postal Code |

Signature (if under 18, a parent or guardian must sign)

## Mail to the **Reader Service:**

**IN U.S.A.:** P.O. Box 1867, Buffalo, NY. 14240-1867
**IN CANADA:** P.O. Box 609, Fort Erie, Ontario L2A 5X3

# READERSERVICE.COM

## Manage your account online!

- Review your order history
- Manage your payments
- Update your address

*We've designed the Reader Service website just for you.*

## Enjoy all the features!

- Discover new series available to you, and read excerpts from any series.
- Respond to mailings and special monthly offers.
- Browse the Bonus Bucks catalog and online-only exclusives.
- Share your feedback.

*Visit us at:*
**ReaderService.com**

RS16R